THE ALIEN WARRIOR'S
WOMAN

GUARDIAN WARRIORS 1

NEW YORK TIMES AND USA TODAY
BESTSELLING AUTHOR

MILLY TAIDEN

THE ALIEN WARRIOR'S WOMAN

Rani Kerf isn't ready to make a love connection. Instead, she's got her mind set on her career. When spying a tall, dark and handsome stranger who takes her breath away while on a mission, her priorities begin to change. But when her team members on the secret operation disappear, Rani goes into rescue mode and discovers the gorgeous alien isn't who he seems.

Tular just met the love of his life. Rani is beautiful, smart, funny, and her acting skills suck. But the problem is he's on a mission and knows that his roguish lifestyle isn't what someone like her deserves in a mate. He has no choice but to let her be the one that got away.

Fate has a different plan for Tular, which includes Rani—that is if she can forgive him for his betrayal increasing the odds of death for each member of her team. So who is this man who's captured her heart, and what does he know about her crew?

—For Tina and Jennifer. You guys are my rocks!

ONE

Rani Kerf could scream and strangle necks right now. She worked so damn hard to make her way in this male dominated job only to be knocked down when someone new came along who didn't know her determination. Or thought since she didn't have a penis, she couldn't possibly do as well as a fucking man.

The Guardians encompassed everything she wanted in life—to help others in time of need, find joy in her job, comradery, and someone else cooking the meals every night. Their mission statement promised the deeds and actions Rani abided by. Well, except for what she was doing at this moment.

She stirred salt, not sugar, into the morning drink that kept the department running, coffee, then snapped the lid on. Just because she was a woman, she was ordered to get coffee for the new chief. He'd learn quickly that she didn't get coffee for anyone unless she wanted to.

All smiles, she joined the men in the conference room, setting the coffee cup in front of the chief and taking a seat. A few of the guys eyed her, most with smiles on their faces, one with a grimace. Sid Booth could kiss her ass as far as she was concerned. Since she started training, she never liked the team leader and vise-versa.

"Okay," the chief said, "let's get this meeting going. Time is short." The men quieted. "Oh, Rani, take notes, chicklin'. You women are good at that."

Her brow raised, but he didn't notice as he looked down at the screen reader in front of him. The same set of eyes as before watched her reaction to the new chief's demeaning words. She didn't want to cause a ruckus here, so she'd give him this once.

Rani took out her comm unit and put it in dictation mode. Setting it on the table, she sat back and listened like everyone else.

"All right, men," the chief started, "we have an undercover mission that is critical. As you have not heard because they are keeping it quiet, Prince Humphrey Leighton of Sathides has been abducted by the Shadowsoul gang on his way to a peace negotiation a few hours ago. The king called the Depleon Guardians because we are one of the best forces around."

"Damn straight," Sid Booth called out. His eyes turned to Rani. "The active duty. Not the trainees, anyway."

Rani fisted her hands under the table. She hated this man. He was the worst excuse for a Depleonian and a jacker. She kept her visage cool, ignoring the comment and keeping her eyes on the chief. She would not let him get to her. That's what he loved the most—getting under her skin and antagonizing her for fun. To get her to quit the force before she barely started. Not happening, dickhead.

She wasn't one of those kickass, badass women she idolized in stories. She wasn't the in-your-face type. Keeping a cool head worked for her.

"Our job is to rescue and retrieve the prince and take him home. Standard procedure," the chief continued. "Last coordinates of Drace Shadowsoul's vessel put it on a path with Nero Terminal in the Varn galaxy. He could've changed coordinates, but that space station is really the best place to transfer their human cargo to another ship and head out to who knows where."

One of the guys raised their hand. "Any specific reason for the abduction?"

"They think it's credits, but don't know for sure. No ransom has been asked yet but give them time. They'll be asking for ganonillians."

Whoa, Rani had never thought about that many credits going to one person before. Did the prince's planet even have that much? She'd bet if she had half that amount, the men wouldn't give her any shit. Nope, her bodyguard would pummel the holy hell out of them for looking at her wrong.

"Everybody in this room will be going, except me," the chief said.

Rani gasped, "Me, too, sir?"

"Of course," he replied. "We need someone to fill out forms and take care of the men." The guys chuckled, knowing how

Rani felt about stuff like that. Sid, on the other hand, growled with a grimace. Damn, she'd be stuck in a cramped ship with his smelly ass. Avoiding him would be nearly impossible, but she'd do her best.

She glared at Sid which sent him into laughter. "You think you can take me on, sweets," he motioned with his fingers to come closer, "any time. Just say the word."

Right, like she was dumb enough to get into a challenge ring with him. The piece of shit was all brute and no brain. As their leader, she was surprised he hadn't gotten the group killed yet.

"Everyone gear up," the chief rallied. "Transport leaves in two hours." Sitting, he finally picked up his coffee.

"Sir," a couple guys blurted. Before they got any further words out, the chief took a sip and spewed it across the table.

Rani, with comm unit in hand, sent the recorded dictation file to the chief. "The notes are on their way to you, sir." She stopped as the chief wiped down his shirt. "Oh, I wouldn't drink the coffee around here, sir. It's horrible."

She walked out, feeling both justified and like shit for the little prank with the coffee. It was sad she had to stoop that low to get a point across. Maybe she was in the wrong profession. Maybe she should quit and do more traditional female things.

She tried laser sewing, but when she accidentally sewed her finger to the pattern, she gave that up. When learning to cook, she set the training room kitchen on fire, and they wouldn't let her back in. Teaching grade school was a great idea until she realized she hated kids who talked back.

In all that time, she never made a love connection. For a while, that was fine because she wasn't ready to be with someone else. She was still trying to discover who she was. In her thirties now, she often wandered about having a family. Maybe if she was the one having kids, teaching them respect and manners for others, she might be able to handle them better. Maybe not. She sighed.

"Hey, Kerf," Sagestar called after her in the hallway as she headed back to her quarters. Gavin Sagestar was one of those great guys who had an adorable two-year-old and beautiful wife. "Don't let Sid get to you." He put his arm around her shoulders. "You know we appreciate you for your brain, not your processing skills."

"I know," she said. "But it's so frustrating."

"We agree and will be there to support you."

"Who's we?" she asked.

Another arm wrapped around her shoulders from the other side. "Me, for one, boss lady," Kase Ironwin said. Ironwin was a crazy kid to her. He was in his mid-twenties and still thought he was invincible. She'd matured past that when she was twelve. But he was brave and had brute strength.

"Thanks, guys," she said. "If not for you all, I wouldn't still be here training."

"We all need someone," Sagestar replied. "We can't take on the universe alone."

"Yeah," Ironwin said, "there's no *I* in team, but there is a *me*." He laughed and pulled away before she could get in a friendly punch. That was so him.

"See you on board," Sagestar said as he stopped at the door to his quarters.

Ironwin bounced on his toes in front of her, throwing air punches. "Wanna work out a little before we leave?"

Working out was the last thing she felt like doing. "No."

"Come on, Rani. Don't be a wimp," Ironwin said. "You asked me to help you get better."

She did ask him for help with self-defense and offensive movements. The academy only taught the basics, letting the students improve at their own pace during their first year. Or in her case, not at all since nobody wanted to work with her.

"Yeah, okay," she answered. "Be there in ten minutes."

"Great!" Ironwin ran down the hall, hands in the air like celebrating a win of some kind. She shook her head. Crazy.

As she stood at her door, Sid stepped into the aisle, looking both ways, seeing Ironwin on one side and her on the other. His eyes narrowed at her and she ducked into her room, locking the door behind her. What was his problem? She had a feeling she would find out soon.

TWO

Opening the station's gym doors, Rani stepped inside and was slapped with the stench of sweat socks. How fucking nasty could these guys be. She wondered if the place was ever cleaned or if the atrocious scent was ingrained into the wall and floors.

Scanning the area, she saw Kase hitting on another female. The girl must've been new as he tried to meet all the females coming through the ranks. The newbie dropped her water bottle and Kase snatched it up and handed it to her. That was nice. Then again, he was able to get a lot closer to the girl when he handed it back which he took full advantage of, running a finger down the female's delicate bare arm.

Rani thought it was time to save the woman before she got trapped. "Ironwin," Rani yelled, "leave the poor girl alone." Kase jerked around at hearing his name. His cheeks were flushed as if he was embarrassed being caught talking with someone of the opposite sex. Bashful was not him and Rani almost laughed.

She couldn't blame the guy. The girl had the perfect body, long, wavy dark hair, and a toothy smile. Everything Rani didn't have. If she were honest with herself, she could stand to lose a few, or several, pounds. Maybe wear her hair in something other than a tight bun. And of course, clothes that fit instead of a size or two too big which was how she liked them.

Right now, she wore a faded T-shirt that hung straight down, no skin-tight tank top. Her shorts were tied with a lot of string left over after tying the bow and baggy around the hips. She had no makeup on while Miss Gorgeous over there looked like a doll. She'd bet the woman even had on that lipstick that plumped the lips. The kind that didn't only make lips *look* plumper, but actually plumped the lips itself. The process was all scientific on how it created the collagen to fatten the area, but it worked.

Kase finally walked away, probably after exchanging numbers. He smiled that adorable smile of a teen boy who got laid at prom. So excited and eyes flashing with life. Thinking back through her life, she didn't think she had ever been so jubilant over anything.

Ironwin slapped his hands together and rubbed them. "What're we doing first, boss lady?" She had no idea why he called her that. She had never been the leader of anything.

Before she was ready, Kase lunged at her, throwing his fist at her face. Rani panicked seeing a huge knuckle sandwich headed her way. Without thinking, her arm swept to the side, knocking away the incoming missile, then stepped forward, delivering her own punch to his stomach.

Kase bent in half and fell to the floor. "You got me, girl. I'm dying, done for, stick a fork in me 'cause I'm turkey."

She laughed at his last phrase. "It's put a fork in me because I'm *done*. Not a turkey, you turkey."

"Maybe, but it took the frown from your face." Rising to his feet, he winked at her. Rani could only shake her head at his antics. If she weren't ten years older than he was, or twenty years older than his mentality. . . "That was a good defense. You didn't even know you were doing it, did you?"

She shrugged, but it was the truth. Her instincts and practice kicked in before her brain did.

"Now," he said, "give me your foot." He held his hands out.

Like she was that stupid. "Why?" she asked, one eye narrowed.

Kase laughed and turned his palms to her. "I'm not doing anything silly, I promise. I just need to see how high your side kick is." He was tall to go with his huge muscles. She wouldn't reach far up on his body. Then again, the most sensitive parts weren't high up either.

She pivoted sideways and brought her leg up, knee straight, heel leading. Her kick landed in such a place that Kase bent and staggered back before she made contact. "Careful there, boss lady. I plan to have kids someday. But that's good for the enemy." Sweat broke out on his forehead. "How about we do hand-to-hand now? Much safer for the ol' crown jewels."

Rani laughed, slapping her hand on her chest. He was serious when he said it, yet he wasn't.

"Okay," he said, bouncing on his toes again, "I have a knife and I'm going to stab your eyeballs and ears."

She got into her defensive stance, then stood straight at his words. "What the hell you talking about? My eyeballs?"

He slashed his arm down, aiming for her chest. Again, she swept his arm to the side then stepped forward for the punch in his stomach. But instead of landing the hit, he grabbed her forearm and twisted her backside against him, wrapping his hands around her throat.

And shit, did he squeeze. She needed to remind him this was practice, not real. Her hips slid sideways, and her hand snapped back, stopping before hitting the crown jewels. Ironwin released immediately and fell away.

"Not doing a great job of protecting those things," she said.

Smiling, he climbed to his feet. "Nah, I think it's more like you can't keep your hands off them."

Her mouth fell open and she pushed him over. "I can't believe you said that." Her face was hot enough to melt. Her eyes darted around, checking if anyone was paying attention to them. Kase laughed harder. "I think it's time for me to go. Neither of us are in true workout mode." She looked him up and down. "One of us has his mind on getting into a particular brunette's pants."

He gasped and said, "Rani, I didn't know you liked women."

She rolled her eyes. "Can it, horny toad." Really, it was ironic. If she were into females, she probably would've had a lot more sex than she had with men. The last man she was with was many months ago. Could've been a year. Man, she needed to get laid. She had to think back to how many times she'd changed the batteries in her "little friend." Her friend took the edge off but she needed the real thing. It had been too long she realized.

On their way out, Kase held the door for her and asked, "Are you as excited as I am about this mission?"

Her shoulder lifted then fell. "I don't think anybody could be as excited as you if they won the Galaxy Lotto."

"Aww, come on, boss lady. You're no fun," he whined, placing his arm around her shoulders.

When she turned to look at his face, she had to lean back so her nose wasn't in his hairy armpit. It sucked being short, but it kept the crown jewels within reach. Goddamn, maybe she was addicted to his balls.

Or she was thinking about her lack of sex life.

She answered, "You heard the chief, Ironwin. I'm there to do piss ant work, stuff nobody else wants to do."

He was quiet for a minute. She waited for his smartass comeback. He said, "A lot of times, you have to take what you're given. But be ready when the opportunity arrives for you to prove who you really are."

Rani stopped in her tracks. "You're not Ironwin. Who are you and what have you done with him?" A serious and philosophical remark was unexpected and surprising from him.

He pulled her shoulders to him and hugged her. Rani wasn't sure what to do.

He'd never done this. Then he kissed her head. "Don't worry, little sis. I'm here and will always keep you safe." Quickly, he added, "And if you're ever attacked by a mob of clowns, go for the juggler." With that, he slipped into his quarters, laughing.

"Thanks, Ironwin," she hollered through the door. "I'll be sure to do that."

She trekked toward her room on the station, Kase's silliness still in her mind. When she stepped inside, she instantly knew something was wrong. Someone was in her room.

THREE

Standing in the entry of her living quarters, lights off, Rani flattened her back to the closed door. She felt a presence even though she didn't hear anything. Pivoting sideways, she kicked her leg out just like in the gym a few minutes ago. If nobody was there, then good, great. But if someone was. . .

Her foot hit something soft and yet hard. Completing the movement, she came back to her stance and flipped the light switch up. Several feet in front of her, Sergeant Sid Booth stood bent over with a hand on his stomach. Pure hate radiated from his eyes. What the hell did she ever do to him? Not one damn thing. She wanted to ask what his problem was but didn't have the balls to do it.

Instead, she dove into the kitchenette and grabbed a big knife. "Get out of my room," she said, her voice shaking.

Sid straightened and smiled an evil grin. "Why, Rani, I'm just here to congratulate you on making the mission." He held his arms out like he was saying *see, I come in peace.* Ha. She knew better than that.

Both hands squeezed around the blade's handle, she repeated her words. "Get out of my room." The panic swept away the ability to make sentences. Her heart beat so hard, it hurt. His eyes drilled into hers, trying to intimidate her. It was working.

A knock came from the door. "Rani, you in there?" Sagestar.

"Come in!" she shouted.

Sid stepped back, eyes narrowed. "This isn't over," he said.

She lowered the knife behind her. The door opened, and Gavin froze mid-step. He looked between the two of them.

"If I'm interrupting," he said, starting to

step back—

"No," she hollered, "the sergeant was leaving. Come in, now."

Sid grabbed the door, snatching it from Gavin's hand and flung it wide. Booth was gone in a flash, no departing words. When her guest turned to close the door, she slid the knife away on the counter. Last thing she needed was Sagestar asking questions.

She didn't want others thinking she was weak or over-dramatic when it came to Sid's taunts. He was nothing but a bully. She would deal with him on her own. Besides, how did she expect to become a great Guardian if she ran to others when a challenge arose?

"Hey," he said, coming forward, "you okay? What was he doing here?"

She plastered on a fake smile. "He came to congratulate me for getting on the mission." She pulled a water bottle from the fridge, keeping her hands as still as she could. "Wasn't that nice of him?"

"Rani," Gavin said, "why would he do that?"

She shrugged, opening the bottle and glugged. She couldn't think up an answer that would satisfy him. Her brain wasn't functioning yet.

"Well, I came over to see if you wanted to get something to eat before we leave."

She gestured at her gym clothing. "I gotta shower and stuff. I'll catch up with you later."

"K." Sagestar gave her a chin pop and headed out. She sealed the door behind him.

* * *

With everybody on board, the freighter launched into space headed to the same coordinates as the Shadowsoul ship a few hours ago. The spatial area was small since they had real cargo in the hold. It was impossible to move around without bumping into someone.

In the tight zone behind the flight crew, the team had gathered to go over the mission details. Sid moved the men ahead of her, effectively keeping her at the back of the group where she couldn't see anything. At least she could listen.

The motherfucking son of a bitch. She wanted to cut him down to size, show him he was wrong in assuming she couldn't do anything useful.

"Listen up, men. We'll be at our target location soon. Based on our contacts' intel, Shadowsoul and his men changed course after leaving our star system. We think he's on planet Nastreon where he feels the most comfortable in his stronghold.

"We are going in as ship workers loading and unloading the cargo from this ship. We'll venture out of the space port shortly after docking. Sagestar, I want your team to set up reconnaissance in the hills east of the port. I will take the rest and split up to blend in and make our way to Shadowsoul's basecamp."

The sergeant pushed a button on his comm unit and a holographic map of the stronghold floated in the air.

"There are two entries to the underground cells where we think Shadowsoul would keep the prince. One is in the main house. The stairs are behind a normal looking door outside the bedroom. The other is through the guards' building." Sid pointed to a structure to the side of the home. It appeared to be a small warehouse with metal siding and not much protection from the elements.

"We don't have intel on what the inside looks like, but we're assuming it's the same—stairs behind a door or a wall maybe." He pushed another button and the image disappeared. "I expect this to be an easy extraction taking very little time. I'd like to be home in time for dinner." A soft chuckle went through the group.

Sid tilted his head up and locked eyes with her. "And you, Kerf, will do whatever I tell you to do." A couple guys snickered, but that was it. The rest remained silent, heads down.

Rani leaned against the door frame, arms crossed over her chest, anger flaring hot. She had a choice here: either be a smartass and earn more hatred or drown him in over-obedience so he felt off balance.

"I am at your service, Sergeant Booth, ready to do any menial job you need." A mix of both choices seemed best. A head bobbed, and laughter was hidden behind a cough. She kept her serious poker face to show she really meant what she said. Whatever. And wouldn't you know it, the dicker head still glared at her. Damned if you do, damned if you don't.

"Dismissed," Booth growled, not taking

his eyes from her. Ironwin was at her side, blocking her view of Sid, or rather, blocking Sid's view to her.

"You know," Ironwin said, "I think your comment went right over his head. He probably thought you were being totally submissive and that messed with his brain."

Rani smiled. "I try. Do you have any idea why he hates me so much?"

Ironwin looked around and scooted her to a corner in the cargo area. "I heard that in training camp, a woman beat him out for a position. The heads of the Guardians were getting shit about not having enough women in the ranks."

"Was she hired just because she was a woman?" Rani asked.

He smiled. "That's the funny part. She actually did better than him in many of the categories."

"So she deserved the position based on her skills and abilities, and jacker head couldn't handle it," she replied. Kase nodded. She shook her head. "Wonderful. A misogynist. Exactly what I needed."

"Aww, no need to worry, boss lady," he

winked, "Sagestar and I got your back." Too bad the rest of the team didn't think that way.

On the overhead speakers, the captain informed they were preparing to dock.

Kase said, "Let's go. You can sit with us."

"I'll be there in a minute," she answered. "Go on." She needed a second to pull herself together, to put her emotions in check and steel her heart. When she got home, she'd need to take a hard look at herself to see if this was where she wanted to take her life.

Shaking off the bad vibes and taking deep breaths, she headed toward the front section of the ship to strap in for landing. But just before stepping out of the cargo hold, a hand wrapped around her neck from behind and yanked her backward between containers. Another arm slid across her waist and pulled her tightly against a body.

Her panic held at bay, knowing it was fucker head and that he couldn't do anything to her with so many people around.

Hot breath blew in her ear. "Did you try to make a fool of me in front of my men?"

Booth asked, his fingers getting tighter. She could still breathe, but barely. His arm around her waist pulled her flush against him. "I have to admit, you do feel good. Very good."

Rani was about to puke, feeling him getting hard against her ass. He continued. "You should be home where you belong, flat on your back, popping out male babies for our future." Then his hand found its way to her breast. That was it. He'd crossed the line.

She shifted her hips to the side and sent a fist hard and fast to his groin. He released her when he doubled over, grabbing his balls.

"Let me make this clear, Sergeant. If you ever touch me or even get close to me again, I will uncrown the jewels." She stepped back when he tried to reach for her. She smirked. "Looks like a woman just bested you once again." Her steps quickened, seeing his face turn into a raging bull, nose flaring and saliva drooling out one side of his mouth. Yup, time to go.

She hurried through the rows of containers and slammed into Gavin. "Whoa, there." He caught her around the shoulders.

"Where's the fire?"

"It's nothing," she replied. "Just Sid being his usual ass self."

"You need me to do something?" Gavin asked.

She shrugged. "Can if you want, but I already knocked his balls out of bounds." She slowed her breathing and the anger pulsing through her veins.

"I'll pass. You got it covered. We're getting ready to dock. Let's get you strapped in." Gavin gently pushed her in front of him and followed her into the main cabin. She sat next to Kase and pulled the straps down, locking them in after fiddling with the damn latch for a minute. Someone needed to fix that. Hands in her lap, she squeezed them together to keep them from shaking. Yes, reevaluating her career choice was definitely a good idea.

FOUR

When the ship touched down, latches clicked open and the men stood from their seats. Booth came from the back, barking for the team, not her, to make sure their deckhand clothing was in place and comm units tucked securely in a pocket.

"Sir," one of the members said, "can we eat before going into the field?"

The sergeant raised a brow. "Yes, good idea. I am hungry." From his bag, he pulled out a handful of rupples from their planet, Depleon, and stuffed it in his pocket. Rani wanted to tell him it was a bad idea to use something that told what planet they were from. Depleon was known as the headquarters for the Guardians. There were no secrets about where they lived and trained.

He turned on her. "You stay here and watch the ship until the captain gets back. Then I want you on comms, *listening*. I don't want to hear a word from you."

With that, the men exited the ship, leaving her by herself. She checked out the food cache the ship had and regretted not taking up Gavin on his invite to eat earlier. There were nut bars, grains, and pre-packaged meals in foil. She flipped through the selection and discovered why those packs were there. Nobody wanted to eat them.

With a sigh, she schlepped into the cockpit to watch the goings on in the bay through the portal. Yup, looked like a busy port. Crates moved here, containers moved there. Robots pulled trains of loaded carts to and fro. And what do we have here?

A man carrying a case looked out of place. He was dressed as a worker, acted like a worker, but there was something. . . The air about him was different. More refined, more nimble. And he was frigging good looking from her view. Damn, he had a great ass that filled out his pants nicely. His broad chest and narrow waist had her licking her lips.

Wait. She was drooling over a guy. She'd never done that in her life. Wow. She stared at him on the bay floor. He was too far away to get details like the color of his eyes, but that didn't matter one bit. She'd do him even if he didn't have eyes. Well, that sounded wrong. He needed eyes, but he didn't need them for her to hump him. Hump seemed such a crude word—

But that was exactly what she wanted to do, if she weren't on a mission she would have considered making his acquaintance in a very intimate setting. Just looking at him had her so wet, she could get off just by watching him swagger across the bay floor.

Shit. She had to get a grip before the guys returned from the eatery. Getting in one more glance at him for nightly fantasies, she saw he was looking at her. Shit, damn, fuck. She jerked back, sliding off the co-pilot's seat and getting stuck with her leg jammed between seats. She had to wiggle her way free without bumping something that would activate the ship. That would be just great.

Crab-crawling out of the cockpit, she

needed to find something to do. First, she fixed the defective latch on the seat she sat in during docking. Then she found a box of broken comm units. Taking them apart, she reworked the wiring or glued together broken pieces. After those, she readjusted the lock on an interior cargo door to open easier.

Looking around the empty ship, she wondered how long it had been since the guys left. Couldn't have been that long if the captain of the ship hadn't returned yet. She picked up her comm unit from the seat next to her and pushed the home key. Seeing the time, she nearly dropped it. Two hours had passed.

She radioed the leader. He didn't reply. She tried again, and again she got no return acknowledgement. Surely, he'd answer no matter how pissed he was. This wasn't a game of who could hold out the longest.

But what if something happened to them? *All* of them? Not very likely. She just needed to be patient and wait. It was just taking longer than the originally planned.

Unable to sit, she paced the small space. The walls were closing in with each pass she made. After half an hour, her nerves were about to make her scream. Something happened to her men. Her only choice was to leave the ship and search them out. May the gods help them if she was captured too.

FIVE

Dressed in a T-shirt taken from Ironwin's bag, Rani left the ship in hopes of finding her men. She had no idea where to start. The port area was a mixed bag of shops, boutiques, and tourist traps. Everything a person could want could be found in the area. That included some really weird stuff she'd never seen before.

When her stomach growled long and hard, she decided to stop at an eatery to get a quick bite. She couldn't focus with her stomach constantly complaining. Scanning the signs above the stores, she saw a familiar logo and headed that direction. Even though it wasn't the highest quality of food, it wasn't too bad. She could do worse.

Stepping inside, she noted the place was empty. Being past the normal eating time, she took that to mean everyone had eaten and left and not that the place was so bad that nobody ate there. To be on the safe side, she'd stick to plant-based foods and nothing exotic.

Rani slid into a chair at a table where she could see the entrance, but she would be inconspicuous. The waitress handed her a menu and asked what she'd like to drink. Rani ordered a tea that was boiled to kill anything in it. That would be the safest beverage. When the waitress sniffled, Rani glanced at her.

With a red nose and glassy eyes, the waitress kept her face tilted down but not low enough that Rani couldn't see. "Do you know what you want?" she asked. Apparently, the waitress didn't want to make two trips. Rani ordered an open-face sandwich with vegetables and sprouts. Not her favorite, but she wouldn't develop a sudden bout of the runs. How embarrassing would that be if she stunk up the entire ship on the way home. The thought almost changed her mind about eating. But her stomach objected.

When bringing her tea, the same female

attendant was nearly in tears. Rani's heart went out to her. She caught the name on the uniform. "Jordyna," Rani said, "that's a pretty name." Apparently, that was not the right thing to say. The young lady burst into sobs, covered her face with her hands, and fell into the chair next to Rani.

Rani sat there not knowing what to do. A stranger had never stayed with her and bawled their eyes out. She put a hand on the heaving shoulder beside her. "There, there, now." Well, damn, she sounded like her mother. That was a scary thought. But what else did you say to a crying adult? Don't drip snot on my fork?

What the hell. In for a rupie, in for a rupple. "What's wrong, sweetie?" Rani asked.

The woman wiped at her eyes. "Nothing." Rani now understood how men felt when they asked a female that question and got the same answer. Maybe a different tactic was called for.

"Tell me who hurt you and I'll go kick their balls into their shoulder blades for you."

The waitress laughed through her tears and took the napkin that had the silverware wrapped inside. She blew her nose, making Rani cringe for a moment, then took a deep breath. "I'm having a bad day," she said. "Nothing I do is good enough for the bitchy boss. Even when I do it perfectly, she finds something mean to say. I'm tired of being dumped on."

Rani could sympathize with her wholeheartedly. "Why don't you find another job?" Seemed obvious to her.

"Seriously?" the lady said. "There are no jobs here. I was lucky to get this. If I quit, my baby would starve."

Rani sat back in her chair. This was a different story now. Rani never had such responsibilities tying her to work. She had enough money saved that she could go a few months without a job if she had to. That was the emergency fund.

"What other skills do you have that someone hiring would pay to get?" Rani asked, trying to be helpful.

The attendant's face turned serious and she leaned in closer to Rani. "You know, I've always thought certain people would pay for the stuff I know."

Rani smiled, leaning a bit away from her new friend. "That's good. Being smart is a start."

"No," the woman leaned closer and tapped her head, "not what I've learned, but what I've overheard."

"Ohhh," Rani got it now. "You mean like being a spy?"

The waitress's face lit up and she sat straighter, thank the gods. Rani was about to fall out of her chair from leaning away. "Yes, a spy." Her eyes darted around like she was checking out all the patrons for. . . who knows? "Others come in here and talk like I'm deaf and stupid. Like I'm not there. Mostly those from other planets. I speak the top three languages of this area. And I hear it all."

Wow, Rani thought. She could barely speak her own language, much less two others. "How do know so many?" she asked.

The waitress shrugged. "I grew up in a neighborhood with a bunch of others from different places. We learned how to speak to each other picking up things. Mostly street slang."

Not only could the woman speak the various tongues, she sounded authentic and not like she learned it in school with all the proper rules nobody ever talked with.

The waitress leaned close again. "Like just a few hours ago, this group of dockworkers dressed in clean, new uniforms walked in and sat down."

Could those be her guys? She kept her mouth closed, letting the story continue.

"They seemed like all the others, except for one obnoxious turd," the lady said. Yeah, Rani could guess who that was. "He treated me like I was born to bow to him."

Rani smiled. "I know just the kind you're talking about." *And his name.* But she kept that to herself.

"I know, right? Anyway, I knew something was up when they paid with Depleon rupples."

Rani startled in her seat. The waitress picked up where she left off. "Yeah. Depleon is where the Guardians are from. Everyone knows that. And with Shadowsoul kidnapping the prince—"

"Wait," Rani said. "How do you know that?" She didn't think anyone knew except her team. It was kept quiet, hoping the rescue wouldn't be expected so quickly.

Jordyna tapped her head again. "I hear things."

"Is the prince on this planet, then? How cool is that?" Rani asked, hoping not to sound suspicious.

"Yeah. Shadowsoul has him at his place. Probably locked up in his dungeons."

Rani nodded, her eyes wide like someone starstruck and not someone taking mental notes, which she was. "So what about the dockworkers?"

Her new friend smiled. "You see, they weren't really dockworkers. They were Guardians in disguise."

Rani slapped a hand on her chest and gasped. "No way."

"Oh, yes," Jordyna said, nodding. "My boss called up Shadowsoul's men and told them."

Whoa. That threw her. "Why would she do that?"

The waitress's eyes narrowed on her. "You're not from around here, are you?"

Rani's heart jumped into her throat, ready to burst from sudden fear. "No. My boss, he has a meeting and told me to stay behind and watch the ship. I wasn't allowed to go with him." Rani hoped by dumping on her own boss, the woman would sympathize with her and feel a comradery of being dumpees.

Jordyna snorted. "Been there," she said. "Everyone around here has a setup with Shadowsoul. They tell him things he might want to know, and he pays them for the intel. Pays well, even." Anger passed over her face. "That's why I was mad earlier."

She looked around the area and leaned closer to Rani. "I told my boss about the rupples then *she* called Shadowsoul. His payment just arrived, and the bitch kept it all. Didn't share any of it with me. She wouldn't have known if I hadn't said something." Rani saw the anger build quickly and understood why. "That money would've paid for my baby's medicine for months."

Now, anger rose in Rani. She didn't think she had any maternal instincts, but they burst forward upon hearing this. Then she remembered her guys.

"So, what happened to the Guardians?" she asked. "Were they captured?"

Jordyna snorted. "There was a huge shootout in the middle of the plaza—" Rani gasped again, but this time it was real.

"When we came out of hiding, everybody was gone. No Guardians and no Shadow men."

That could only mean one thing: her men had been taken by force. "Wow," she tried to fake excitement, "I bet that was scary for a bit."

"Huh, you bet," the woman said.

Rani had to think quickly. She was running out of time and she needed to get details about this Shadow guy without making the waitress suspicious. "How would a person go about getting to Shadowsoul's place?" Too obvious?

Jordyna's eyes widened. Yup, too obvious.

"Why would you want to do that?" Her voice stuttered a bit.

Shit, damn, fuck. Rani smiled innocently. "Well, actually, my boss runs a news agency and he's always looking for a story. And if I could get him a meeting with Shadow man, then he might give me a promotion. Or a raise even."

Her friend sneered. "Don't count on that. But if you want to talk to Drace, he usually goes to the bar a few buildings up when he's home. Otherwise, the main road takes you past his place."

"Drace?" Rani asked.

"That's Shadowsoul's first name," she said. "I hear he can be a nice guy when he wants. Well, I heard that once. I know he likes the ladies."

"Really?" Rani said.

"Yeah, he's always picking up someone at the bar, I hear." A ring came from the kitchen. "I need to go." She rose from the chair, tears gone. "Your food will be ready in a moment."

Rani let out a big breath and dropped her face into her hands. What the hell should she do? They never went over the scenario where the team was captured and only she was available to rescue them. She was sure the thought never crossed Sid's mind.

Sid would tell her to call for backup and then go home. She'd ignore that last part but contacting HQ would be good.

"Here's your food, miss." Jordyna set the plate on the table. "And I want to thank you for listening to me. I appreciate your concern."

Seeing that she had no choice when the waitress plopped her butt in the chair, Rani smiled and said, "No problem. It was nice to meet you." Jordyna started to walk away but turned back. Her eyes searched the room again and she looked over her shoulder.

"A word of advice," she whispered, keeping her head down, "all the communications in and out are monitored by Drace's men. Careful who you contact and what you say."

Rani gave the waitress a nod of thanks, guess her own acting skills were worse than she thought.

Now what? She couldn't contact the Guardians without tipping off the bad guys. She knew nothing of the area or terrain.

Movement from the a nearby table caught her attention. A man was coming her way, smiling at her. Hold the phone. Shit, fuck, damn. It was the dockworker she fantasized about an hour ago.

SIX

Rani sat at the restaurant's table, staring at the man who made her want to come. Holy crap, this could get embarrassing. Up close he was even better looking than she realized. Rani kept reminding herself to breathe and not drool. She couldn't remember the last time it happened in real life. Rani realized she must've been quite distracted with Jordyna since she never saw him walk in and sit down.

His mouth moved but she didn't hear the words from her heart pounding in her ears. She held the plastered smile on her face and stared at him.

"Well?" he said.

"Well what?" she replied.

His smile grew bigger. "I asked what you are eating. It's looks really good."

Rani snapped back in her seat. "Oh, this thing?" She glanced down, trying to remember what it was called. Hell, right now, she couldn't remember her name. "It's a sandwich."

The guy chuckled and took the seat opposite her. She must have had a sign on her forehead that read *please sit down, especially if you're a hunky cute stranger.*

He said, "Oh, that's a good start. That narrows down the menu to the first page."

Rani's brain finally kicked in after she started breathing again. "Silly me," she laughed. What the hell did she just say? Could she be any more lame? "It's a scythe bloom and peet wafers."

His smile wavered a bit, only noticeable if watching closely. "Sounds delicious," he said. "I thought about getting the iglinger."

"That one is great at home," she replied. "But here, I don't know where the meat comes from, and this being my first time here. . ." She shrugged.

"You are so right. You must travel a

lot." He raised a finger to signal a waitress. Jordyna came over.

"What can I get you, sir?"

"How about the same as. . ." Rani stared at him as his sentence trailed off, looking at her. It took a second to realize he was trying to get her name.

"Oh! Rani. My name is Rani." Damn, from her training manual, she knew she should've given him a fake name, but what the hell?

"As Rani," he finished. Jordyna turned from the guy and gave her a *you go, girl* wink. If only, she thought. His attention was solely on her. "What brings you here this day, Rani?" he asked.

"The food," she said, still smiling like an idiot to keep her cover.

He nodded, seemingly amused. "I meant what brings you to Nastreon?"

"I'm here on work. You?"

"I'm here for work too. Just started the other day on the cargo bay floor," he answered.

He was a working man, which she already knew from seeing him working. She wanted to kick herself for being so stupid. She took a deep breath and let it out, then picked up her fork and knife to cut into the open-faced sandwich.

"You okay?" he asked. Was that genuine concern she felt coming from him?

"Yeah, just settling in," she answered. "I never got your name."

"Sorry about that. I'm Tular."

Good gods, could he be any more perfect? Even his name was sexy. Hell, he could've said it was Penelope and she'd would still swoon. But she noted he didn't give her a last name. Only certain people did that. People like her who had something to hide. They chitchatted about nothing until his food arrived. Then were quiet for a bit as he ate too.

Even though she wanted to take him back to the ship and maul him, she had to make plans to rescue her guys. Plus the cargo bay wouldn't be the most comfortable place to jump him. First, she needed to scout the area to see what she was up against. Did Shadowsoul have men on the ground? He had to since his guys arrived so quickly to take down her team. What else was out there? She wouldn't know until she got outside.

Tular set his fork down. "How about I give you a tour of place? The weather is really nice out."

She contemplated his invitation and didn't see any harm in it. Plus, she'd look like a normal person walking around with someone else and she could add more fodder to her nightly sweet dreams. That was a very good idea. "Sure, I'd love to."

His smile grew and teeth shined, just like a crocodile before it ate you. This was not the time to drop to the table and beg him to take her.

"You both done?" a different waitress asked. "This one or two checks?"

"One," Tular said.

"Two," Rani said. Then she realized the only money she had was rupples. She gave him a sigh. "Fine, but I'm paying you back."

"Sure," he said and rolled his eyes.

She slapped at his hand playfully. "Hey, I mean that. I don't like being in someone's debt."

"Don't worry," he said, eyes sparkling, "I won't take advantage of it." Rani froze in her chair. She needed to change her underwear. They were soaked from his sexy look. She chanted in her head: Rescue first, over and over.

After taking care of the bill, he placed his hand in the small of her back and guided her out the door. No one had done that before. At first it felt awkward, but she grew to like it. Like it a lot. He was closer than a stranger should be, but her personal space didn't feel invaded. He felt comfortable to her.

When they passed the night club the waitress said Shadowsoul visited a few buildings from the café, she made a mental note since she planned on going there tonight. She needed to check out the enemy to see what defenses he had. Maybe follow him home and sneak in, find the stairs and rescue the guys. Easy peasy.

The weather was great. Sunny, but not too hot. Cool breezes filled with flowery perfume, no wonder Shadowsoul chose to live here. She would. As they talked, she once again had that feeling this man wasn't groomed for the cargo area of an out-of-the-way planet. His hands were rough, but fingernails were clean. His speech was full of slang, but it came out sophisticated with no accent to hint at his heritage.

"Where are you from, Tular?" she asked.

He seemed flustered at the question, then said. "I'm not from anywhere anymore."

"Ohh, how cryptic," she teased. "Mystery man." She glanced around the area. One main road ran down the center of several buildings. A few looked like shacks ready to fall down. Not many people walked about. There was probably a reason for that.

He laughed. "Unfortunately, it's true."

"How can that be?" she asked. "You were born somewhere."

His hands left her back and shoved into his pockets. She immediately felt the loss of his touch and wanted to tell him to put it back. But his sudden melancholy concerned her.

He continued. "I'm kind of a black sheep. My family has a business, I guess you could say. And when I made it clear that I didn't want any part of it, they shunned me and told me not to ever come back."

"Even your mother?" Rani asked. She couldn't believe a mother would turn against her own son for not wanting to follow in his father's footsteps.

He shrugged. "I don't know. She wasn't there when Dad and I had the final go-around. He ruled the house and told me he didn't want to see my face again." He let out a sigh.

"I'm sorry for bringing up sad memories, Tular."

The side of his lips raised. "That's fine. It's part of who I am. Besides, it happened years ago. Many." He kicked a rock and she bit her tongue, wanting to soothe his pain away. Her heart hurt knowing she'd done this to him.

Then he grabbed her arm and dragged her next to a tree. "You see that man with the long coat?" On the sidewalk in the distance, a man walked. She had to squint to see his coat was long.

"Yeah?"

"That's one of the Shadow men," he whispered. Why he was being quiet, she didn't know. The guy was far enough away that he probably couldn't hear them if they yelled.

"How can you tell?" she asked, looking for what was different with the man. This was something important.

"His coat," Tular said. "Nobody wears long clothes unless they are hiding a big gun. Shadowsoul's men carry big guns."

Of course! It was hot as balls outside. She should have thought of that right away, but having seen some people wearing strange clothes, she hadn't focused on it.

When the man turned his head in their direction, Tular gasped and slammed his lips over hers. It was so sudden, she stood there shocked for a moment. But it didn't take long for her to figure it out. For some reason, Tular was disguising their presence as a couple in love out for a stroll.

And who was she to complain? Hell no. She'd practice her acting skills right now.

Rani wrapped her arms around his neck and he backed her against the tree. Pressed against her, he felt so good. His body fit hers perfectly. His hard spots rubbed her soft spots, and one of his spots was growing harder.

She opened to him and he dove in, tasting her, wrangling tongues with her. Her heart pounded. Never had she been kissed like this. Not even by the few guys she dated for several months.

When he let her breathe again, she panted. He laid his forehead against hers. "Sorry about that," he said. She wasn't. "I didn't want the Shadow man to think we were spying on him."

Words hadn't form in her brain yet, so she just nodded. He smiled down at her. "You kiss very well," he said in a low, growly tone.

Her panties were wet again. She nodded and squeaked out the word "Acting."

His smile faded a bit. "Of course. Your skills at deception are quite good."

Rani bit out a laugh. "I wouldn't say that."

"No?" he asked, voice like silk. "Seemed real to me." He stood close enough that she felt his body heat. Boy, was he hot. Her pulse picked up. Then he stepped back. "Sorry, I, uh, didn't mean to crowd you." Hell, she didn't mind. In fact, she loved being crowded. It took everything in her to not grab his shirt and drag him back against her body.

Why couldn't she find someone like him

on her home planet? But who said she had to live where she grew up? She could live here. Giving up the Guardians would be tough, but she bet he could make her forget all about them.

Another guy in a long coat came along. He ducked and took her hand. "Let's get back to the port. My lunch hour is over."

His hand holding hers, he guided her through the maze of alleys to the restaurant. He was quiet the entire walk. Had she said something wrong? Hell, she could barely talk after that kiss.

He stopped and turned to her. "Can I see you later?"

Yes! she wanted to scream, then realized she now had the general layout of the small town and needed to prepare for the rescue. "My boss and I are leaving soon. He said he wanted to be back before dinner." Which was true.

He ran a finger under her jawbone. Sadness shone in his eyes. "Got it." His hand pulled back and slid into his pockets. "Well, it was nice to meet you. I have to be going." He turned on his heel and headed toward the landing bay.

SEVEN

Rani stood in the middle of the plaza watching the only man she couldn't think around walk away. Her feet wanted to run after him, her voice wanting to call him, tell him she would see him again. That she wanted to be with him. But her head said something else. And she knew her men were in trouble. They came first.

Scanning the shops, she found a glamor boutique with makeup and dresses. That's what she needed. After stepping inside, she was hit with enough perfume that she wouldn't have to wear any for days and still smell like flowers. She waved her hand in front of her nose and coughed. How could they breathe in here?

"Can I help you?" a female voice said. She followed the sound and came across a woman who looked to have walked off the runway. Makeup was painted onto her face, and her clothes were like nothing Rani had ever seen.

"My makeup case was stolen and I need to buy everything," she said. The woman's eyes lit up. How could she even open her eyes with all those lashes? They looked to weigh several pounds each.

"Have a seat right here, young lady, and we'll get you all fixed up."

Yeah, that's what Rani was afraid of. But she needed to go in disguise and look like someone who would garner Shadowsoul's attention. If he would take her back to his place, then she could find the guys and break them out. That was now the plan anyway.

"We always start with a good foundation," the woman said, opening a bottle and pouring a blob onto a sponge. "The great thing about this brand is that it changes color."

"That's normal," Rani said. She had foundation that smoothed out her red, blotchy cheeks.

"Oh, no," the lady said. "I mean it changes color." She put the sponge down after applying a layer and lifted a gadget she'd never seen before. After pushing a set of buttons, the salesperson waved it in front of Rani's face several times, then handed her a hand mirror.

Rani about dropped the mirror seeing her lime green reflection.

"See," the woman said, "changes color."

"Got it. It can change back, right?"

"Sure." More buttons were pushed, waved in her face, and her skin was back to normal.

"You know," Rani said, "I'm not that good with application. Do you have something not so. . .advanced?" The saleswoman pulled out a bottle Rani recognized. "That new one's good. I'll take that." Her face started to feel tight and she stretched her mouth wide, trying to get it back to normal. Then her eyelids pulled back. She gripped the countertop wondering what the hell was happening to her face.

"Look," the woman said smiling widely, handing her mirror again, "See how this formula tightens and lifts the skin?"

Staring in the mirror, that wasn't how Rani would describe it. Her eyes looked bugged out with her lids so far up. Her cheekbones stuck out like a skeleton's while her cheeks were sucked in. And her lips stretched farther across her face. She wanted a disguise, and she got it.

The cosmetic specialist continued on, stroking mascara onto her lashes that increased in diameter and length. Good thing her lids were pulled back or you couldn't see her eyeballs under the thickened hairs.

Next came blush, which Rani didn't normally wear. Then white, shiny powder to "highlight" her natural features. Her nose was kind of wide across the bridge and down the length, but there was nothing she could do about it and had accepted herself as she was. Nothing on her was perfect, but she was happy with her body image. And the man who married her would have to be okay with it, too.

The woman pulled a few tubes of lipstick and studied the colors against Rani's face. "I think this one goes best. Open up." Rani dropped her jaw a bit for the woman to apply the red color. As she painted it onto Rani's lips, she continued talking. "Now, this brand is really good. It plumps up your lips to give that pouty look men love." She stepped back to examine her work.

Rani said, "Yeah, my lips are kind of thin. Appearing larger would be good."

Again, the saleswoman gave her that look. "Oh, no, honey. I mean this actually plumps up your lips." That's when Rani felt tingling around her mouth. She felt her lips getting puffier and stretching. If she looked down, she could see them growing.

She almost went into a panic, wanting to wipe it off with the closest fabric. She wasn't used to something enlarging itself on her face. "Here, madam." Rani took the mirror a last time. She closed her eyes, afraid of the results.

Peeking through her forest of lashes, she caught the glimpse of a beautiful woman she'd never seen before. Her eyes widened to being extra bug-eyed. "Wow." When her lips moved, it felt like she had been hit in the face and they swelled up. She opened and closed her mouth several times, getting used to them.

"You look fabulous," the saleswoman said. Well, yeah. She didn't look anything like herself. "Anything else you need?"

Rani was almost afraid to ask. "I need a couple dresses and shoes."

The attendant clapped her hands together. "I have just the thing for you."

Oh gods, that really worried her. No telling what would come out. Maybe something that made her taller. That would be cool. Being short was a bummer. Or maybe it would make her boobs bigger. She looked at her chest. Nah, she didn't need that. She liked her C-cup. But this was what Drace Shadowsoul liked.

The saleslady strolled from the back, material draped over her arm. At least the dark blue was a pretty color. Rani slid off the stool to go try on the dresses. But when the salesperson stepped behind the counter, she put the dresses in a bag.

"Shouldn't I try the dresses on?" she asked.

"No, no. The dresses will fit."

Rani found the opposite to usually be true. "Maybe just real quick to check the length."

"The dresses will fit."

"But—"

The woman sighed. "You don't know anything about all this, do you?" Rani shook her head. Shopping wasn't a favorite past time, and the fancy stuff wasn't her. "The dress will adjust to you when you put it on. It will fit."

Now she got it. She'd heard about clothes like that but had no need for such items.

"Here are your shoes."

Rani looked at the one box on the counter. It was long and narrow like a shoebox, but there was no picture or size posted. The lady caught her staring at it.

"I supposed you'd like to try these on too?"

"Yes?" Rani wasn't sure she'd get her wish, but it was worth trying. She did not want to walk around in shoes that pinched her toes. Plus, what if they were ugly?

The woman took the lid off and Rani gawked at the contents. She didn't even want to know how this worked. The lady poured half of the box contents into the box cover. It looked like clear snot sliding from one container to the other. She had to close her eyes to keep from getting sick.

The woman put the boxes on the floor and stood back. Rani looked at the goo and then up to the lady. Then it clicked, and she blurted, "I have to put my feet in that?"

The saleslady threw her hands into the air. "You wanted shoes. I give you shoes."

"You gave me snot in a box."

The woman laughed. "Yes, it does look like that. Now, put your feet in and stop whining."

Rani untied her issued boots and slid off her socks. Hovering her foot over the goo, she couldn't make herself do it. Then the woman pushed her shoulder and Rani fell forward, having to put her foot down to keep from falling. The mud-like material squished between her toes and around her foot but didn't stop there.

It continued up the side of her foot and higher on the back of her heel. Then before her eyes, the goop formed the shape of a shoe and solidified around her feet, giving her the perfect fit. All she could do was gape at it.

"See," the woman said, "it will fit."

Rani lifted her foot from the box to see

a three-inch heel on a buff-colored shoe that flexed with every movement. Incredible.

"Do you want to try the other one?"

Rani shook her head. She was a believer. Now she worried about how much all of this would cost. She probably didn't have enough in her emergency savings to begin to cover the price. Plus, her credits were Depleonian. Why didn't she think of that?

The woman set a slip of paper before her with a number on it. Rani had to be looking at it wrong. The amount was reasonable. She glanced up at the lady. "That's it?" she asked.

"Of course," came the reply. "I didn't offer the good stuff since I didn't think you could afford it." This wasn't the good stuff? Damn, she was really out of the fashion loop. She'd never seen any of these things on her planet. But she never went to the fancy stores either.

Rani had to come up with a reason for the credits being Depleonian. "I, uh, just spent my vacation time on Depleon. All my credits are still in that form. Do you take that?"

"Of course, credits are credits."

Rani pulled paper denominations from her purse and handed them over. She even got back change in the form of the planet's monetary type. That would be good if she had to buy something small. She didn't have much left.

Hurrying back to the ship, she'd never had so many people stare at her before. It was nerve racking even though they were staring for a good reason.

Back on the ship, she checked her comm unit. No messages, no attempted connections. Nothing. She wondered if Drace would kill her guys right away or torture them until they died. Both thoughts stole her breath. She knew these guys. They had been her family for several months. She'd never forgive herself if they died because she didn't do her best to rescue them.

Digging around in her bag, she pulled out a comb, hair pins, and her magic weapon she purchased when she started training with the Guardians: her deadly butterfly clip for dangerous missions.

The barrette had three prongs that slid into any hairstyle. One prong contained a sleeping agent, one had truth serum, and the third had deadly poison. A prick with any prong would deliver instant results. She'd never had to use it before, but she never knew.

She lifted the blue dress and it resembled a material trash bag. Oh, gods, what did she get talked into? She didn't want sleazy, but she didn't want humiliation either. She slipped it over her head, hoping for the best.

As soon as it settled on her shoulders, the fabric shrunk in some places and expanded in others. Just like the shoes, the dress fit perfectly. She looked fabulous, amazing, and nothing like herself. An awesome disguise.

Standing, staring at herself in the reflection of the chrome walls, she told herself she could do this. She was strong and brave and could have a nervous breakdown after her guys were back on the ship.

Then the thought crept into the back of her mind that chances were very high that these would be her last hours of life. She pushed the thought away. If she were to die tonight, then it was for a worthy reason.

Just in case, she left a diary entry on

her comm unit so someone would know what happened to everybody.

65

EIGHT

Rani walked into the nightclub and looked around. She'd been to one once when she was in advanced learning with a bunch of girlfriends, but never on her own. She didn't care much for places where you had to yell to talk to the person next to you.

The late hours hadn't arrived yet, so the crowds were small and relatively quiet as well as the music. To calm her nerves, she took a stool at the bar and ordered a fruity drink. Keeping her hands wrapped around each other hid how shaky they were.

The barkeep was a beautiful woman about ten years younger. She wondered if the girl had any of the magic makeup on. Nah, her beauty looked natural.

"Here ya go, fruity on the rocks," the barmaid said. Rani thanked her and set the proper credits on the bar. The woman scooped the money and gave her a side glance. "I haven't seen you before. You new or just passing through?"

"Passing through," Rani replied. She tipped the glass to her mouth, and not used to her newly plumped lips, a bit dribbled out the side. She quickly wiped it from her chin and the bar top.

The keeper smiled. "You got that lipstick that makes your lips fatter?"

Rani glanced up at her, fear swirling in her chest. Was her cover blown already?

The keeper laughed. "Don't worry. I see it all the time now. Haven't tried it myself. You like it?"

Rani felt like someone had glued donkey lips over hers. "They take some getting used to."

"They look great on you." The girl picked up a cloth and wiped down the bar.

Rani thought back to Jordyna from the restaurant. "So, I guess you see a lot working here, huh?"

She snorted. "Some things I've seen and

heard, people would kill to know."

"Really?" Rani leaned over the bar as if talking about conspiracy. "Like what?"

The barkeeper looked her up and down and shrugged. "You don't look like the dangerous type."

Rani laughed. "Believe me, I'm not." She put her hand out. "I'm Rani." Well, shit. There she went giving her real name again. These undercover gigs didn't seem to be for her. She'd have to stick to the straight forward, first-on-the-scene, help-those-in-danger situations. Not things where she had to lie.

"I'm Arbelle," the girl said.

"That's a pretty name," she said with little thought.

The keeper smiled. "Thanks. It's my grandmother's name." She looked around and leaned closer to Rani. "A couple nights ago, I heard whispers about abducting some king's son. I don't know if it was true or not, but that was pretty big."

Rani feigned shock. "Wow, that is big. Hope it's not true."

Arbelle smirked. "Knowing Shadowsoul, it was true."

Rani's eyes got bigger, not that her bug eyes weren't already huge. "You know of Shadowsoul?"

"Of course, everyone here knows about him. He's good for business and bad for everything else."

"How so?" Rani couldn't imagine anything good from a bad guy.

"He's good when he's in a calm mood and brings all his people. They spend a lot of credits, tip really well, and usually don't cause problems. Plus, his farm provides most of the food around here."

"You mean the restaurants and bars?" First off, Rani couldn't believe a supervillain would have a farm. Something just wasn't right with that.

"Yeah, but that's not all good," Arbelle answered. "He charges a lot for the produce and doesn't let anyone else bring in what he supplies. Someone tried to offer competition and the family disappeared. Never seen again. He doesn't take kindly to others who cross him."

"Obviously," Rani replied. That added to her already thin self-confidence about pulling this off. "How long have you been working here?" she asked.

Arbelle grunted. "Too long."

"Why don't you find something you like to do?"

The bar maiden sighed. "Jobs don't come easily here. I'd leave for a bigger city, but my boyfriend took all my money when we broke up. I have nothing to my name for a while."

"Oh" was all Rani could come up with. The girl must've been devastated. But she knew a plethora of individuals who would pay well to know what the keeper heard. She'd bet the king would've paid a small ransom to have known what was planned for his son.

"What would you do if you could do anything?" Rani asked.

Arbelle looked away for a moment as if dreaming of her perfect life. "I'd like to help those who have been wronged. Those who need someone to make things right. Like hunt down my ex and take back what's mine."

"That's really noble," Rani replied.

Arbelle laughed. "I wouldn't call it that as much as I've seen so many bad things happen to good people and I want that to change. Fight for those who can't." Rani thought that was beautiful. This woman had a huge heart and she had been wronged. She wished she could do something to help. But who was she? A nobody. "Excuse me," Arbelle said, "I need to get back to work."

Rani looked around and was surprised by how many people were there. She'd been so enwrapped with Arbelle, she didn't notice anything else. She sipped her drink, being careful not to drool again. These lips would be the first thing to go when she got back to the ship.

She glanced around the crowd, wondering if Shadowsoul and his men were there. There weren't any big groups, so she doubted it. She watched the women at the tables. Some with a guy and others were in small groups. They were all smiling and laughing, many very loudly from drinking a bit too much.

One group with wrapped gifts on the end of the table were doing shots, guffawing and nearly falling off their chairs. On the count of three, several threw their heads back. Everyone slammed their drinks except one gal who missed her mouth, splashing half on her face, the other half down her shirt.

The lights lit up more of the dance floor and the music was cranked up to the decibel of a spaceship revving its engines. So much for an enjoyable time.

Then everything seemed to stop, and heads turned toward the entrance in slow motion. Among a group of men dressed in all black, a tall, charismatic man in shaded glasses and bright gold jacket and pants walked in. Who was this guy? He looked gaudy.

Arbelle rushed down the length of the bar toward her. "Rani," she huffed, "you should go before he sees you."

"Who? That guy?" She nodded toward Mr. Flashy-in-a-bad-way.

"That's Shadowsoul and his men." Arbelle came around the bar and grabbed her hand, hauling her through the crowd.

"Where are we going?" Rani asked, looking back to get another view of the man she wanted to talk to.

"The ladies' room. You need to stay out of his sight."

"Why?"

Arbelle shoved the door open and dragged her inside. "Because if he sees you, he'll ask you to go home with him."

"I'm not that kind of girl," Rani said, even though that was her purpose for being there. Maybe she should've thought this through a bit more.

"He won't care, Rani. If he wants you, then you are his. And you look like his kind of woman. Pretty and breathing. Plus the women are never seen again." Arbelle paced a moment. "Wait for him to settle in. He always sits along the wall next to the side door. Go around the other side and leave."

"Leave?" Rani couldn't do that. Her men depended on her getting them out. She took a second to think things over. Her training, so far, had never gone into crazy rescue missions of the rescue team. What was the right thing to do? She took a deep breath and calmed herself.

If Shadowsoul was here already, then her men were either locked up and waiting to be interrogated, or dead. If he hadn't killed them yet, he'd probably wait until after he slept off the booze tomorrow. What did that mean? She'd have time to find the guys then.

But if she went home with him tonight, she'd have to sleep with him. Chills ran through her. The idea was not pleasing. She wasn't the kind to have sex with just anyone. She had to feel something for them, like there was a love connection. Her heart always went into the act. She couldn't keep them separated. But for her team, she could do that. No, she couldn't. Yes, she could. No, she couldn't. Shit, damn, fuck.

"I'll stay here for a while," Rani told the barkeeper. "Then I'll go."

Arbelle's shoulders relaxed. "Good. I've got to get back." With that, the cute barmaid was gone.

Rani paced where Arbelle had a moment ago. What was she going to do? Her courage had taken a nosedive seeing her new friend's fear. Shadowsoul was a bad guy, but he looked dumber than deadly dressed up like a statue dipped in gold paint.

But he was deadly. He killed without thinking. No heart. And the women he took home were never seen again—murdered seemed the more likely case.

She didn't like the idea of using her feminism to entrap a man, but men would, if they could, and fail. Why? First reason was that few men were good looking enough to pull it off, and second, women weren't stupid enough to fall for it.

Dammit, she was doing this for her men. Adrenaline and determination coursed through her and she threw the door open. Chin held high, she sashayed from the ladies' room, searching for the idiot resembling the sun—too bright to look at. Coming to the front half of the club, she hadn't seen Shadowsoul yet. He wasn't where Arbelle said. Instead, she saw Tular headed toward her.

Panicking, she turned and pushed through the crowd. He would recognize her and blow her cover. Then she'd never get to her team. She scooted around people, between people. When did this many get here? She'd been in the restroom for a minute. A group standing in the middle of the walkway busted out in laughter and one of the guys stepped back, nailing Rani in the shoulder with his body.

She stumbled back, trying to grab onto anything to keep from going down. Her damn high heels didn't help any, but her feet were the most comfortable they'd ever been. She plowed through a couple guys with their backs to her, then bounced against a table and into someone's big, strong lap.

She looked up to apologize and saw the man she wasn't sure she wanted to meet holding her. Drace Shadowsoul.

NINE

Rani sat on Drace's lap in the nightclub, staring at his surprised, but happy face. She flustered, not knowing what to do. Any resemblance to a plan shot out the window along with her balance.

Drace reached up and pushed her jaw closed. "What a lovely young lady we have here."

She sputtered, trying to say a dozen things and getting nothing coherent out. She stretched her legs dangling off his lap, trying to reach the floor. This was one of those times when being short really sucked. When she tried to scoot off, his hand came down on her outer thigh, holding her in place.

"No need to leave so soon, my lovely," Drace said. She nodded and he laughed. He ran his hand up her thigh, fingers slipping under her dress. She slapped her hand on his, stopping the movement.

"Let's dance," she blurted. She yanked his hand from her leg and rolled off his lap, grabbing the table for balance. Her eyes searched for Tular while she dragged the deadliest man she ever met to the far corner of the dance floor where she was sure Tular wouldn't see her. She straightened her arm and put it on her partner's shoulder. He laughed and jerked her against him.

His laugh was deep. His words tickled her ear. "You're such a shy one," he said. "Who would've thought with your looks you would be that way."

"What?" she said, glancing down at her outfit. It was sexy, but not trampish. The skirt fell just above her knees and her entire chest was covered. But her back was bare and the material dipped low. "I think I look nice. Nothing is hanging out. If you don't like—"

He laughed at her again. "Hold your tongue, little one. I meant no mean words. It was simply a compliment."

"Oh," she replied. "Then thank you. That was very nice." He laughed again and swung her around. His smile was brilliant. Almost as bright as his jacket.

"I haven't laughed so much in a very long time. You amuse me," he said.

Great. She'd always wanted to be a clown.

"Come home with me tonight," he said.

She gasped. Damn, he moved quickly. Now that she was head to head with the reality, she couldn't do it. Her stomach roiled at the thought of him on top of her pounding away. "I thought I made that clear. I am not that kind of girl." His eyes darkened at her rejection. His hand squeezed her waist, fingers biting. "But I will come over tomorrow and plan on staying the night." Did that just come out of her mouth?

He stared at her like he couldn't believe she'd said that. "All right then," he said. "Invitation accepted." Rani let out a small sigh. "But you'd better be there, or I will come looking for you."

"I'll be there bright and early," she replied. He released his hold on her and snapped his fingers high in the air. He headed out the door, his men rushing to catch up. One of the men, an older looking guy, snarled at her. Reminded her of Sid. Wonderful.

Rani stood, breathing deeply, trying to figure out what just happened. She'd delayed her execution at least until tomorrow. She still had tonight to live.

In almost a daze, she made her way to the bar and fell onto a stool. Arbelle came to her. "What happened? I told you to stay away from him."

"I tried," she said, "but I tripped." If she decided to stay in this job, she needed to take high-heel-walking lessons.

Arbelle poured her a shot of clear liquid. "Drink this," she said. "It'll calm your shakes."

Rani swallowed half then slapped her chest and opened her mouth to suck in air. "Damn, what is this?"

Arbelle smiled. "Good shit, that's what it is."

Rani scooted the shot glass forward. "Filler up." The barkeeper laughed and tipped the bottle.

"Will you be all right here on your

own?" Arbelle asked. "I wouldn't go home yet. Let Shadowsoul get far away in case he decides to wait a minute to see if you leave." Rani nodded. Good idea, she thought. Then she spotted Tular in the crowd.

"What do you know about him?" Rani nodded toward him.

"The really cute one?" the keeper smiled at her. Rani felt her face heat. He was really cute and was a great kisser. "I've seen him around a few nights now. I think he's new here or something. I haven't seen him leave with anyone or even talk to a female for that matter. He just saddles up to the bar and has a few drinks, walks around, then leaves."

"Strange," Rani said.

"Agreed," Arbelle said. "You stay there for a while and I'll be back to check on you. Understand?" The woman pointed a finger at her and smiled.

"Yeah, got it. Anyway, if I tried to stand, I'll probably fall flat on my face." Her legs felt like the goop she stuck her foot into to make her shoes.

Keeping to herself, she relaxed to let her pulse and breathing return to normal. Now she had to come up with another plan to deal with tomorrow. She tossed back the shot, coughed, and stared at the imitation wood on the bar.

She'd need to get there early, before Drace woke and decided to kill the Guardians. He hadn't drunk much, so there would be no sleeping in for him. Hopefully, they would get to a place where she could use the sleep serum in her butterfly clip on him. That would give her time to find the stairs leading to the lower level cells.

A shot glass filled with clear liquid was place beside her on the bar. She looked up to see Tular staring down at her. Shit, damn, fuck.

TEN

Tarrek watched as a beautiful woman led Shadowsoul onto the dance floor. She looked a little familiar, but someone with that face, he would remember. The woman wasn't his type—too much makeup and bling. If he wanted that, he could've stayed home with his family.

No, he was a simpler man. Didn't like fake people. Wanted everything to be straight up, full transparency. Of course, his father couldn't allow that in the business, so Tular got out. Quite unceremoniously at that.

Resembling every other single man there, he leaned against the wall in front of Shadowsoul's table and stared at the dance floor. He knew if he were to overhear anything, it would be tonight. With the boss away, hopefully the minions would play. And talk among themselves, they did.

He heard bits and pieces over the music. He didn't want to move closer and look suspicious, so he strained to get what he could. They talked of prisoners, plural. They were probably referring to those Guardians they caught in the plaza earlier today. He wasn't sure how Drace found out about them. They seemed like normal dockworkers to him. Just like he seemed to be a normal dockworker, which worried him.

Suddenly, the men left en masse, and walked out the door behind Drace. That was quick. He looked around for the girl the man danced with. He finally saw her at the far end of the bar talking with the female server.

He found his feet walking toward her; his subconscious must've been telling him something. There was something about her that drew him, even though she was totally wrong for him. What the hell? He wouldn't glean any further information from the Shadow men tonight, might as well enjoy some female companionship.

He couldn't remember the last occasion he spent time with a woman. In the beginning, when he was young and stupid, having just broken from the family, he hooked up with a number of females. All one-night stands, of course. That was understood going into the bedroom. Neither party would see each other the next day or ever. That was how his life was going to be.

Hadn't changed much except his hook-ups dwindled to nearly non-existent. Somewhere down the line, he'd changed. The satisfaction he once got from solitary night partners wasn't enough anymore. He craved more than what sex alone gave him. He often wondered if he'd lost his mind or if that was normal for someone his age.

He ordered two shots and walked toward her end of the bar. She looked deep in thought. Her face carried worry and fear but was still elegant with all the makeup. He set the glass on the bar next to her. She looked up at him and froze.

He thought she was going to bolt. Her expression showed surprise, happiness, and dread. All that just for him? He almost laughed.

"Hey, beautiful," he said, "may I join

you?" She stared at him a moment longer. Her eyes were stunning. He felt like he'd seen them before. Maybe in passing somewhere.

"That would be nice," she said. His heart raced as he pulled a stool closer. Sweat broke out on his forehead. What was wrong? Sure, the woman was stunning, but she wouldn't cause him to have a panic attack or anything. He slammed back his drink and held up a finger for another one. She took the glass he set on the bar for her and did as he did, coughing afterward.

For some reason, he was glad she wasn't accustomed to alcohol. She wasn't a bar babe then. Though he didn't think she was.

"My name is Tular." He glanced at her, waiting for her name. Instead of speaking, her eyes got wider than what they already were. Was he that scary? "Look, I'll go if you—"

"No, no," she said, laying a hand on his arm to keep him there, "you're fine. I'm just. . .just. . .not myself right now." He'd take that reason. Her touch sent his blood rushing to his head and not the one she could see. "My name is, uh, Arbelle." She looked down at the bar and shook her head.

"Arbelle is a pretty name."

She laughed. "I thought so too."

That was an odd thing to say, he thought. One look at him and she laughed harder. He caught her when she almost slipped off the stool, laughing. The male bartender filled his shot and he tossed it back. He was starting to feel a bit better.

"So, Arbelle," he said, "how many drinks have you had tonight?" If she was a sloppy drunk, he didn't want to waste time on her. He'd had enough of that over his last seven years.

She calmed. "I'm sorry," she said. "This is a humorous moment for me. I drink very little. Tonight is unusual."

He asked, "Do you come here a lot?"

"This is my first time here and on the planet," she answered. He nodded and played with his shot glass on the bar. "What about you, Tular? You come often, looking for a woman to take home?"

He glanced at her due to her audacity and laughed at how cute she was. Under the face paint, he could tell a pretty face lived. And her voice sounded familiar.

"No," he answered. "I just started working here at the port. And, nah, I'm too old for one-nighters anymore. I've moved on."

"Moved on how?"

Good question. "Well, I've grown up, I guess. I've been on my own for a while and have learned what's really important in life."

"And what's that?"

He laughed at her interrogation. "You're very curious, you know." She shrugged and smiled. "Your smile is pretty." He thought her lips were too big, but he was too much of a gentleman to say that to her face. He'd been slapped by a female for less.

She blinked at him. He wondered how she kept her lids up. They looked heavy.

She said, "You avoiding the question?"

Question? Oh, right. Something about her drew him and he lost himself in her. "The important things are family and finding the one partner who's made for you."

"You found that partner yet?"

He sighed. "No, but I met someone today who intrigued me. Something about her reached out to me and dragged me to her table." Then I wanted to drag her to the nearest bed.

"Table? So why aren't you with her?"

He glanced down at the glass his fingers fiddled with. "She was only passing through. Left for home soon after we met."

"Today?" she said, her hand clenched on his forearm. He raised a brow at her. "Never mind. Did you get her contact information? Maybe visit her."

He smirked. "I was so caught up in her that none of that entered my mind. My brain shorted out, I guess." Too much blood flowing south for coherent thoughts. Especially after the hottest kiss he ever had.

"Awww, that's so sweet."

He laughed. "Maybe, but I hope I'll see her again." He let out a big breath. "I'd never felt with a woman what I did with her. And when I kissed her, I knew she could be the one."

Arbelle bounced in her seat. "No way," she said. "Really? Tell me more."

A laugh belted out of him. "She was beautiful, kind, smart, and completely lied to me about who she was."

Her hands flew over her gaping mouth and she *eeped*. It was cute. She asked, "How do you know? Did her acting skills suck?"

He smiled. "She said something about acting too. Must be a thing with you women."

She eeped again and nodded. "It is. With every woman. Yes." He chuckled at her strangeness. He'd never met anyone quite like her. She continued, "So if you saw her again, what would you do?"

He'd grab her close, kiss her until they had to breathe, and lock her in his bedroom and keep her there until she agreed to be his. "I'd get her contact information certainly." His emotions were becoming too much. Knowing he let her get away was enough to push him into a dark place. The lights mellowed, and a slow song played over the speakers. "Would you like to dance?"

"I'd love to," she gushed. He took her hand and led her to the main floor. Instead of keeping his distance, he pulled her flush against him. She wrapped her arms around his neck, holding on like she didn't want to let go.

He couldn't believe how good she felt against him. She fit him perfectly. Maybe he'd been hasty to think Rani was the woman for him. Arbelle pulled at his heart. She smelled wonderful. He wanted her. He wouldn't let this one get away. He leaned down and placed a kiss behind her ear.

She stiffened for a moment then seemed to melt into him. He took another taste of her skin. So good. His heartbeat picked up, fueled by her silent encouragement. He started to get hard from her sexiness. He worried he'd scare her off with too much too soon. Trying to pull away, he was surprised when she wrapped an arm around him and pressed against him, including his groin.

His excitement exploded through his veins. His passion was too hot to take anymore. "Would you like to see my place?"

"Yes," came immediately. She must've been feeling the same about him. Someone to meet his passions and desires.

ELEVEN

Without another word, he stood, holding onto her wrist, and then led her out of the bar to his vehicle out front.

Less than twenty minutes later, he pulled into a driveway leading to a house and parked. She studied the area. "Is this your place?"

He nodded once. "I thought we weren't getting to know each other."

Fair enough. She held up her hands. "I'm a curious person. Besides, I was just trying to start conversation."

He led her into the house in silence. She didn't push for more conversation. She was here for one thing. Hot, mind-blowing sex.

When they reached the living room, he turned and faced her. His eyes held hers for a few moments and she thought she saw a flash behind his irises. He lifted a hand and cupped her cheek then moved it to the back of her neck, pulling her closer. Dipping his head, he claimed her lips.

The kiss was soft, almost exploratory at first then he deepened it, thrusting his tongue into her mouth. She groaned. Wrapping her arms around his neck, she closed the gap between them, pressing her body to his. Hot need rushed through her, igniting to wildfire deep within.

He wound his arms around her waist then ran his hands down her back to cup her ass. He lifted her off the ground and she instantly wound her legs around his waist, hooking her ankles behind him.

Their tongues danced and twined around one another. She rolled her hips, grinding against him. They had too many garments between them. "Clothes. off."

His response was a grunt as he walked them to the stairs. She could feel his hard length through his pants. Each step he took rubbed it against her. Desire was lava in her veins.

He was not unaffected. She could tell he struggled to keep it together most likely to make it up to his room. His arms tightened around her and his fingers bit into her ass cheeks. Small, throaty moans came from him as he walked.

When they reached the stairs, he broke the kiss to nip at her earlobe. She let out a soft groan and gripped his shoulders. He took a couple steps, then cursed before lowering her on the step.

Too fast for her to track, he had her dress yanked over her head and tossed on the tread behind him. He stared at her hungrily. Desire filled his depths, darkening his eyes. "So beautiful."

His words uncurled a raw hunger of her own. It was only one night. She didn't need the complications of a relationship.

He unfastened her bra, then pressed a kiss to the top of one breast before taking the nipple in his mouth. She moaned and arched her back, pressing into him. Pinpricks of pleasure scattered over her skin as he teased the sensitive bud.

Her panties dampened and her pussy throbbed, begging to have him deep inside her. She didn't need teasing. She wanted out of control, hot, mindless fucking. "I need you inside me now."

* * *

Tular's cock jerked at her command. He'd had plenty of one-night stands but none like this. He intended for it to be a quick fuck. But when he kissed her, his plans went out the window. It may only be for one night, but he was going to savor every inch of her.

"I should make you beg."

She let out a strangled groan as her reply and he chuckled. He kissed his way down her body, nipping at her skin along the way. When he reached the top of her underwear, he bit down but not hard enough to break the skin. After all, he didn't need to mark her. He wasn't ever going to see her again.

With a swift jerk, he removed her underwear and settled between her thighs. Her arousal intoxicated him, making him want things he knew he couldn't have. Pushing the thoughts away, he leaned forward, covering her with his mouth. Her hips jerked.

He licked and sucked, savoring every sweet drop of essence. After slipping two fingers inside her, he pumped while he teased her clit with his tongue. Soft sounds of pleasure came to her as she rolled her hips in rhythm of his hand. He slipped a third finger inside, stretching her and finger fucked her.

Her breathing turned into pants when he increased his rhythm and bit gently on her clit. She cried out in pleasure as her orgasm washed over. Her body jolted with each wave of her release.

After a final lick from entrance to clit, he stood and removed his clothes. Settling between her thighs, he gripped his cock and rub the head between her folds, teasing her once more.

He pushed inside, slow at first, then thrust forward. She cried out and gripped his forearms, her nails biting into his skin. The feel of her milking him as he pulled out and thrust back in again almost pushed him over the edge.

When she wrapped her legs around him, causing him to go deeper, he knew he wouldn't last much longer. "Come for me again. I want to watch you come undone."

"Yes."

He cupped one breast, pinching her nipple between two fingers, then picked up the pace, pounding into her. Pleasure built deep inside him, consuming him. When she screamed another release, every one of his muscles tensed. He thrust forward and cried out as he reached his own climax.

TWELVE

Rani stepped from the automated transport vehicle to see the most amazing villa she had ever seen. She could understand why an unsuspecting female could be swept off her feet and treated like a queen here.

On the ride to Shadowsoul's place, she noticed enough munitions to service an army. No one was getting inside unless Drace wanted them to. She stood at the black iron gate and gazed inside. She wasn't sure how to get someone's attention to let her in. She heard a *clang* and a *clink*, and the gate slid to the side. Easy peasy.

When she stepped through, a big male popped out of the shadows. His face showed no emotion. Either a good poker player or highly-trained soldier. Oh, wait. He was the same guy who last night gave her a nasty look as Shadowsoul's group left the club. She dubbed him Sid II.

"Follow me," he said. He whipped around and marched up the drive.

As she tried to keep up, she took in the various areas. There was a sprawling mass of land with trees that had different fruits, vines with berries, and other shrubs. She heard a lot of noise behind the main house, but the home's grand width hid whatever they had back there.

Eyes were on her from everywhere. She had no doubt weapons were trained on her to fire if she made any suspicious moves. All she carried was a black bag with clothes she lifted from the guys and other necessities. Her butterfly comb was neatly tucked into her hair.

All morning she'd tried to keep her mind occupied with this mission to save her team instead of what happened last night. She had planned on being here much earlier, but it was too hard to leave him. Could a person fall in love in eighteen hours? Somehow, she'd managed to.

Something about Tular drew her to him. She wanted to be near him, touch him. As long as he was in the same room with her, she felt a comfortable peace.

She had to put him out of her mind. If she lived through this next bit, then she'd seek him out, but she was mentally prepared to do whatever it took to successfully complete the task before her.

Before she reached the home's front entrance, Drace stood on the porch watching her, a smile on his face. She swallowed hard. A shot of clear liquid encouragement would be good about now. Sid II left her to carry on by herself.

Fluffing her hair to make sure the comb was securely in place, she walked up to him. "Good morning, Drace. How are you?"

He lifted her hand to his lips. "I'm good now that I have such beauty with me." She smiled demurely but was trying not to throw up in her mouth. She had no delusions. He would kill her without a second thought. He laughed, and she didn't know why, but she'd take it as a good sign.

He stepped to the side of the open door and gestured her through. "Please come into my humble home." Rani stepped through the threshold into a magnificent wonder of art and light. She'd seen places like this in travel brochures. But to actually be in one was over the top.

She kept her chin stiff and hands steady. She was proud how well her nerves had subsided since earlier this morning. She felt collected and in charge.

"Would you like a drink?" he asked. "You seem a bit nervous."

Well, shit. She really needed to take spy lessons if she had to do more jobs like this. She played the part of an innocent as best she could. "So soon?" she said. "It's two hours from lunch still."

He chuckled. "Never a better time." They entered a parlor type room and he poured himself a shot and tossed it back.

Ahh, she understood now. He wanted to get her drunk so he could have his way. So typical. Well, she was one step ahead of him. She planned on getting *him* drunk, hoping he would pass out, or be too out of it so she could use her butterfly clip.

"Wow," she said, "I've never seen someone able to handle such a strong drink like that. Bet you can't do that again."

His brow raised. Without question, he poured a second, and a third, and swallowed each in one gulp. After an *ahhh,* he slammed the glasses on the bar top. "Please, allow me to give you a tour of my home." A thin man with sparse hair approached. "Brahr will take your belongings to my room." She handed her items to him with no hesitation. She didn't want him to think she was hiding anything.

With his hand on the small of her back, he pushed her through the main aisle that spanned one side of the house to the other. They zipped past colorful rooms and strange artwork. She noted there were doors in every room along the back side of the house. She figured Drace wanted to get out quickly from a frontal assault.

About the only room they hadn't seen was his bedroom, which she was sure was next. When they came to doors overlooking a beautiful pool, she dug her heels in—which were still the most comfortable shoes she'd ever worn—and stopped.

"So amazing," she gushed. "Let's go outside." She pushed the double glass doors open and stepped out before Drace could do much to stop her. He hollered for Brehr to bring a drink and two glasses. Guess he wasn't giving up the getting drunk tactic. Fine with her.

Just like everything else, the back gardens were stunning. She pulled out a rattan chair from a matching table under an umbrella and sat. Breathing deeply, she let out a big sigh. "This is incredible, Drace. Your home is astounding."

"Thank you. I take much pride in selecting only the most perfect items to be housed within. Only beauty." Brehr set down a tray with a bottle of hard liquor and two shot glasses. Well, straight to the point here. No messing around with low octane wine or bubbly. "This is from my best collection of Gruazzaulph. Very old and very smooth."

She smiled, having no idea what Grazz-whatever was. Must've been from some planet that specialized in making it. He poured a shot for her and one for him. She started to decline the beverage and his eyes flashed in anger. Whoa. On second thought, she lifted the glass. "Here's to drinking before lunch." She tipped her head back and finished it in two swallows. She prepared to cough, but there was no burning in her throat. A heat settled in her stomach, but it wasn't unpleasant.

Surprised, she said, "That's not bad. It actually tastes good for what it is."

Drace leaned back and laughed. She didn't think what she said was funny, but happy was better than those furious eyes.

"Your turn," she said.

He smiled wide. "Are we making sport of this? To see who goes down first?"

"I love a little friendly competition," she replied. "What about you?"

"I love that you love such a thing. This will be quite enjoyable, but short, I believe." He filled both glasses. With his nod, they lifted their cups, clinked them together and tossed them back at the same time.

"So, Drace, your home is fabulous. Do you have a basement?" she added quickly, "to store chilled beverages?"

He burst out laughing while he refilled cups. "I do have rooms below the main floor, but they hold other things." Again, he lifted his glass and both leaned back and drank.

Her head was starting to feel a little dizzy, but he seemed fine. That made five drinks for him? Two for her. She thought back to the women in the bar as they laughed too loudly and swayed in their chairs. Time to call her acting skills again. This would not end well. He refilled the glasses.

"Tell me, my little one, what is your name?" Rani sat back and laughed. All this time and she'd hadn't told him her name. How pathetic was that?

"They call me Rani," she said.

"Well, Rani, here's to new friendships." They both tossed, but Rani threw it to the side of her head instead. She smacked her too fat lips together. He looked at her and laughed. Now he was coming unhinged. She saw it in his eyes. "Tell me, little Rani," he said, again filling her drink, "what position do you like best?"

Position? Did he mean at her job? "Well, the chief position wouldn't be bad, but there's a lot of shit that goes with it." His brows drew down then a belly laugh shook him.

"You are so funny," he replied, "I think I will keep you for a while." Another shot prepared, another shot to the side of her head. This wasn't too bad. He'd be out in no time. Unfortunately, what she'd already drank was having more effect on her. She thought he was funny, too, and laughed with him.

"Drace, I can just see you all tough and macho, killing anyone in your path," she said, no reason why, she just said it and they both laughed like she'd said the funniest thing ever.

"Rani, I can see you under me, screaming my name. What do you think of that?" She stared into his eyes, then both burst out with honking snorts of laughter. They smacked glasses together and drank.

Rani swayed in her chair and sat forward, eyes wide. "Oops, I drank that one."

Drace leaned over the table toward her. "I did too!" More stupid laughing. When he poured, more went onto the table than into the cups, his laughter jerking his arm around.

"Rani," he said, "you should stay away from people like me." He scooted her cup closer.

"I kinda like you Drace, ol' boy," she answered. Damn, this shit was better than truth serum. More snorting and she laughed at him. He slapped the table and lifted his drink high. "To. . .whatever!" She lifted her glass just as high, cheering him on. This time when she threw back, like the woman in the bar, she splashed the liquid all over her face.

Drace dropped his glass, laughing so hard, shattering it on the hard surface. He jumped up from his chair and stumbled sideways. Rani sprang toward him, trying to catch him, and they both rolled onto the ground. Drace lay on top of her and his mouth came down on hers. For a minute, she wanted to visualize Tular, but she remembered where she was.

She turned her head and pushed up on his shoulders. His eyes flashed with anger again. She slid her tongue around her lips, distracting him. "Hey, my hunky man, how about I clean up and meet you in bed?"

His eyes got wide and he stumbled off her. He took her hand and launched her up, throwing her a foot into the air. She grabbed onto him and they both screamed giggles. She dragged him toward the double doors and inside; he'd gotten her into his room.

Holding on to her, he kicked the door shut, losing his balance, but staying on his feet so they landed on the bed. His hands were all over her, but she managed to pull away.

"I need to go to the bathroom," she said. "You get naked and under those sheets." She stepped back. "Be ready for me, baby."

His hand rubbed his tented pants. "I'll be more than ready."

She turned before she got sick watching him fondle himself and opened the first door. The light popped on to a closet. She glanced at him. "Oops, not the bathroom." He slid to the floor laughing. She went to the next door, finding the room she needed. Once inside, she locked the door and leaned over the counter. Fuck, shit, damn. How was she getting out of this?

THIRTEEN

After washing her face of all that makeup, securing her hairclip for easy access, and having pulled her shit together, but still seeing double, Rani exited the bathroom and saw Drace sitting against the headboard, covers over his lap, chest bare. She'd been acting more drunk than she was. But when seeing him, she wished she really was drunk if only to get through this.

She took a step forward, rolling her hips in a sexy, hopefully, seductive way. He watched her, almost in a trance. She was not sure if it was her or the booze that had him like that. Getting the hang of the sexy walk, she came toward the end of the bed, not noticing the rug. Her heel caught the material and she fell flat.

Horrified, she grabbed the footboard and popped up. Drace's wide eyes stared at her, then they both broke into laughter. She climbed onto the bed and crawled toward him. The closer she got, the more he frowned.

"What?" she asked.

"Who are you?" he slurred.

"What do you mean? I'm Rani."

"You don't look like the same Rani."

Oh, right. "I took my makeup off."

He stared at her. "Wow. I need to get some of that stuff for my sister." Giggles erupted again. He leaned forward and dragged her onto his lap. She reached up and took the butterfly clip from her hair and shook it free, all sexy like, swinging her head. When the room started spinning, Drace grabbed her before she fell off the bed. More giggles.

"Enough," he said. "I want you now." He flattened her to him, his lips smashing against her face. His fingers fumbled with the zipper on the back of her dress and pulled it down.

Rani held her hair clip in her hands, trying to pull the safety tip off the end of the sleep agent tine. The damn thing was stuck. That's what she got for not practicing with it. Lesson number one, always know how to use your equipment.

Not able to see what she was doing while trying to keep his tongue out of her mouth, her fingers fumbled the comb and it slipped into his hair. She slammed her hands on his head, trying to catch it before it fell beyond reach.

He groaned. "Yeah, baby. I like it rough." His tongue pushed against her teeth and she clamped her jaw closed or she'd puke in his mouth—booze or him, she didn't know. Both.

Clip in her hands again, she blindly pulled on the end, desperate to get the sleeping agent in him before things got too far. The cap finally snapped off and she jabbed it into his shoulder and held it there. Seconds later, he fell back against the headboard, eyes closed.

Rani slumped with a sigh of relief. She re-zipped her dress, put the comb back in and climbed off the bed. She tiptoed to the door and peeked into the hall. A guard stood not too far away. Bet he loved that job, listening to his employer grunt and scream. Eww.

She closed the door and turned slowly, head spinning a bit. She wasn't nearly as drunk as she pretended. Either her acting was getting better or Shadowsoul wanted sex so badly, he was blind.

Instead of getting to the stairs to get to the bottom level, she'd have to go through the guard's shack. They should all be out this time of morning. Glancing at Drace sitting up, she thought it might be better if he looked to be sleeping.

Quickly, she pulled the covers back, cringing when accidentally seeing his small package. Eww, eww. She tried to scoot him, but the man was too heavy. So she climbed back onto the bed, grabbed his feet, and yanked him down. Back on the floor, she pulled the covers up to his chest and noticed something wasn't right. His chest wasn't moving.

She felt for a pulse and found nothing. She grabbed the comb from her hair and looked at it. The tine missing the cap was the one for the poison and not the sleeping agent. Oh, gods. He was dead. She left him covered and looking asleep and hurried out the glass doors exiting to the pool area.

She'd freak out later on the way home.

Thinking back to the hologram shown in the ship, she looked around the grounds and spotted the building she needed. With no one around, she bee-lined in that direction. Cutting across the grass and dirt, her heel sank into the soft ground and she whirled her arms to keep from falling. Damn alcohol. She still didn't see anyone but workers in the gardens.

Almost to the shack, the sound of a laser gun powering up froze her in her spot.

"Why are you out here?" a gruff voice growled. Sid II. Wonderful.

"Drace is sleeping and told me to get out for a while," she said. His weapon was aimed at her as if he really meant to shoot her. He and Sid really needed to get together. Another of the guards came around the corner of the shack.

"You," Sid II said to the man, "take her into the cells and hold her there until I get back from Clovestea. Then we'll deal with her later if Drace still wants her alive." He smirked. The guard grabbed her arm and swung her around. He hauled her forward and she hit and kicked at him, best she could with a heavy buzz. She was not going into any prison to be killed.

The guard flinched when she kicked his shin. "Ow, stop fighting me, dammit."

Wait. She recognized that voice. "Tular?" she whispered.

"Shh. Be quiet." He jerked her around like he was being rough. She was sure Sid II appreciated that. He led her into the guard building and through a door to stairs leading down. After closing a second iron door, he let her go.

She kicked him again. "What are you doing here?"

He hopped around on his one leg. "I can ask you the same thing." He took his helmet off and leaned against the wall, rubbing his shin. "Do you have to kick so hard?"

"I didn't." She looked down at her shoes. "These are amazing. You've got to get a pair. They literally form to your feet."

"I'll be sure to stop in before I leave," he griped. "So, what happened to you and your boss leaving yesterday?"

"Oh, stop patronizing me," she said. "You said you knew I was lying about everything."

His mouth gaped. "How do you know that? I only told one person."

"Yeah, I know," she said, looking around the musty space, "Arbelle."

"Well," he said, anger rolling in his voice, "your disguises are better than your acting."

She whirled around on him, putting a hand to the wall. "Don't you get angry with me, buddy. Shouldn't you be working on the docks at the spaceport?"

His face sagged. "Fine, we're even. Neither of us are who we said. Now, who are you and why are you here?"

"What about you and here?" she threw back at him.

He got in her face. "I asked you *first.*"

She popped her fists onto her hips. "Fine. My name is Rani Kerf. I am a Guardian. In training."

His brows raised. "I want the truth," he growled.

"It is," she answered. His face contorted. She'd never seen someone so shocked in her life. "Oh, come on," she said, "it's not that hard to believe."

His mouth moved, but no words came out. Finally, he said, "I didn't think girls were allowed in the Guardians."

Her eyes narrowed at him. "We are not *girls*. And have you been living on an asteroid? Women have been in the Guardians for a few years now."

Tular paced and grumbled to himself. "Are you here to find the prince?"

"That's why *you're* here?" she said. "No wonder you knew so much about the Shadow men. What are you? A bounty hunter in it to get a huge reward?"

His face darkened then he turned away. "Something like that. You must be here to free the men captured yesterday in the plaza."

"I am." She looked around again. "If these are the cells, where is everybody?"

Tular sighed. "I was on my way out. Last night, it seems, Drace ordered the prisoners taken to Clovestea and held there."

"Why?"

"He was afraid more Guardians would come and he wanted all evidence of them gone from here. That's what I heard, anyway."

"He doesn't have to worry about that anymore. Or anything for that matter," she said.

"Why's that?" he asked.

"He's dead."

"He's *what*?!" he yelled, his last word echoing through the cavernous space.

She cringed at the loudness. "You don't have to get all riled up about it."

"You *killed* Drace Shadowsoul?" He ran his hands through his hair.

She leaned forward, hands on hips again. "It's not like I did it on purpose. It was an accident."

He paced frantically. "How do you *accidentally* kill someone like Drace Shadowsoul?"

"Like it's never been done before. Back off." Her frown deepened.

His pacing continued. "All right. I have to figure out what to do now."

That was easy, she thought. "We go to Clovestea."

"There is no *we*." He stopped inches

from her face.

She pecked him on the lips with a smile. "That's not what you said last night." His angry expression didn't change one bit, but he backed her against the wall and took her lips with his. His passionate energies surged through her exactly like in his bed not long ago. She wrapped a leg around his waist and he lifted her, back against the wall, other leg around him. He grinded his hard cock against her clit, eliciting tingles in her nerve endings. She needed to find a bed and fast.

Between kisses, he got out, "Why did you leave this morning? Why did you say you'd never see me again?"

"I didn't know how this rescue would turn out."

He put his forehead against hers, both breathing hard. "Not acceptable."

She laughed. "What? You want me to see you even if I'm dead?"

He looked into her eyes. She saw more emotion there than she ever had from anyone. "No," he replied, "I won't let you die. You're going to be stuck with me."

"Good," she smiled, "when are we

leaving for Clovestea?"

FOURTEEN

Sneaking out of Shadowsoul's compound was relatively easy with most of the guards escorting all the prisoners to another planet. Completely sober, Rani stopped by her ship and grabbed everything she thought she could need, changed clothes, and refilled her hair clip with three tongs of sleep agent and no poison this time. She wasn't sure how she was going to explain that to the new chief. Hopefully Drace's death would be ruled natural causes. . .with poison in his system.

Rani climbed on board Tular's smaller galaxy hopper and whistled. "Wow. Bounty hunting must pay well. I'm in the wrong job." Electronics filled every space including the ceiling. No see-through portals existed like in the older cargo freighters. This was top-of-the-line technology.

"Come on up when you're ready," Tular called out from the front. She set her bags in a corner and stepped through the narrow entrance into the domed cockpit. The round room was the strangest control center she'd ever seen. What struck her first was there were no windows; all the walls were opaque black. Like being inside a cave. But a million tiny lights flashed across the control board that encircled the room.

"This is amazing." She drooled over the advanced features she'd heard about but had never seen.

Centered in the room, swiveling completely around, he pointed to the seat next to him. "That's your spot, babe. Copilot."

She carefully sat. "I've never been in a ship like this, much less know one switch."

"You're smart. You'll pick it up quickly."

She looked at the incredibly complicated, incredibly fascinating dashboard lining the curved wall. Right, pick it up quickly. With the back of her seat to his, she realized if she leaned to the side, she could access all the controls on her half of the room. Tular could reach the other half. With the chair rotating in a full circle, she could almost operate the whole ship on her own.

"Strap in," he said. "I'm flipping on the three-sixty."

Rani pulled the straps over her shoulders and locked in. "What's a three—"

Tular touched buttons and the entire top half of the dome disappeared to reveal the hangar bay they were in. She gasped at the changed. "Wha. . ."

"Walls are still there." Tular reached up and tapped the invisible barriers, making a clicking sound against the plasma glass. "Don't look down." Instantly, she looked at the floor. It too had disappeared, showing the docking bay floor. She snatched her feet up as if she'd fall, then slowly put one foot down and felt the flat surface.

"Oh, gods. This is. . .there's no word for it. It's like we're floating in the middle of the bay. You can see everything like there's no walls."

"Latest in plasma projection technology," he said. "Wait till we get into space with just the stars around you. It's an astonishing experience."

She turned to him, smiling ear to ear. "I can't wait."

He looked at her, brushing the back of his fingers down her cheek. "It's not as astonishing as looking at you, having you with me."

That was unbelievably corny, but she loved it because he meant it. He held his hand out, palm up. "You ready?" he asked.

She took his hand. "Ready. Just don't ask me to drive."

He laughed then laid his other hand on the flat console in front of him. Flight control came over the speakers, clearing their take-off. A few taps of his fingers and they shot into the atmosphere, headed for space. A moment later, they broke the binds of the planetary gravity and reached hyperspace where it felt like everything came to a complete standstill.

With nothing around but the pinpoints of light, Rani felt she was adrift in space. She'd never been a religious person, but this was. . .aweing. It was a reminder that some greater power existed even if it had chosen to hide itself. She felt smaller than each twinkle in the distance. Space was so vast.

"Unspeakable, isn't it," Tular whispered.

"It is." She reached out, thinking she could almost touch "it." She spun her seat and watched as the universe revealed itself to her in a complete sphere. "You know," she said, "if I got space sickness, there'd be puke covering the Titan constellation right now."

He laughed. "Got that covered. Under the seat is a stomach evacuation container if the need arises."

She groaned. "Let's hope it never comes to that."

"Agreed," he said, turning back to the control panel. The dashboard came online, lighting up to show all the controls. Tular plugged in coordinates and pushed other buttons and toggles.

"How far behind them are we?" she asked.

"The main group left earlier in the morning. A few of the leaders left not too long before us. Zul was part of that group."

"Who's Zul?" she asked.

"Murrow Zul. He's the one who caught you outside the house. Luckily, I happened to be on my way through. I'd just found out what was going on with the prisoner transfer and was leaving for the port when you showed up."

"Lucky is right," she replied. "And you happened to be in the restaurant when I was, and the night club." She raised a brow at him. "Are you stalking me?"

He laughed and leaned back in his seat. "If I wasn't then, I certainly am now." His fingers diddled on her arm. "It will be a few hours before we arrive." His voice was low and sexy. "I could put the controls on com-pilot and show you the ship."

Rani noted the devious twinkle in his eye. "Yes, I'd love to see the 'rest' of the ship."

He laced their fingers together and tugged her down the hall toward his room.

A whirlwind of desire and emotions fluttered inside her. She could never get enough of him.

Once inside, she released his hand and pushed him to the bed. He chuckled and stumbled backward. When his legs touched the mattress, he fell in a seated position.

Right where she wanted him.

She reached for the button of his pants and when he went to stop her, she slapped his hands away. "It's my turn to play." Raising her brows, she dared him to challenge her.

The corners of his lips twitched, and he fell back onto his elbows, giving her access. She undid his pants and freed his cock. Gripping him in her hand, she slowly stroked then lean in and licked the head of his penis, teasing. He let out a groan, jerking his hips forward, an invitation for her to taste him.

She took him into her mouth and sucked. His low half-growl, half-moan fueled her own desire. It made her want him all the more.

He fisted his hands in her hair and pulled at the roots. A groan broke from her throat. He moved his hips, sliding his cock in and out of her mouth. She cupped his balls and rolled them in her hand as she sucked.

His hips bucked and the muscles in his thighs tensed underneath her arms right before his body jerked and he came. She savored every drop of him.

He gripped her arms and pulled her up to him, capturing her mouth and pushing his tongue inside. Her pussy ached for him, needing him.

With a quick twist, he flattened her back against the mattress and ripped open her shirt. Buttons flew off, bouncing on the bed and the floor. Her pants were next along with her panties. Within moments, she was bare to him.

A low growl escaped him as he stared down at her as if he loved what he saw. He bent her legs so her feet were flat against the mattress then spread her knees, exposing her to him. Starting at her knee, he kissed his way down the inside of her thigh until his mouth was on her, licking her, pleasuring her.

Desire turned into sensations, a bliss covering her inside and out. She lifted her hips to grind against his face. He moved with her, intensifying the pleasure until she exploded in wave after wave of an orgasm.

Standing, he yanked his shirt over his head, tossed it to the floor, and then removed his pants fully. "Roll over and get on your hands and knees."

A thrill shot through her and she

quickly did as he commanded. The anticipation of him taking her from behind almost made her come again.

The mattress dipped as he climbed on the bed and positioned himself behind her. He guided himself inside, stretching her. She let out a moan as he filled her to the hilt. He gripped her hips as he thrust in and out over and over, going deeper and deeper. Surge after surge crashed over her.

He flattened a hand to her belly, then slid it lower until his fingers teased her clit. He rubbed in circular motions, escalating her pleasure while he fucked her from behind. Her climax tore through her and she screamed out in pleasure as she tumbled over the edge. Moments later, he joined her in his own release.

FIFTEEN

Tarrek couldn't help but smile. He hadn't been this happy since he left his home planet and family so many years ago. At first, he hadn't missed them. He was furious with his father and older brother trying to trap him into a job he had no desire for. In truth, he hated all it encompassed.

Now, of course, he saw things through eyes ten years older and a millennium wiser. He understood the politics behind what they thought was right, but to him, wasn't worth it. He knew he could do more, serve more, on his own. And that's what he had done.

"Cracker?" Rani asked. They sat

together in his pilot seat, her between his thighs, snuggled tightly against his ever-hardening dick. She was in a T-shirt and nothing else. How could he not be hard? He opened his mouth and she shoved in a square.

His fingers bounced along the console and a hologram of the planet Clovestea popped up. It rotated slowly, showing them the full terrain.

"It looks so green. Like it's all wilderness," she said.

"The only things I know about Clovestea," he stated, "it has massive animals that eat anything that moves, and they have an old prison that was once the most feared place by criminals."

"Why most feared?" she asked. He opened his mouth and she stuck in another cracker.

"Because if anyone escaped, they would more than likely be eaten before they got anywhere safe. Supposedly, the smell of blood drives the creatures into a bloodlust and they rampage."

"Bummer," she said. "Then how are we getting to the prison?"

"The civilization has their complete existence underground in tunnels," he answered. The holo changed from the image of the world to a map of a maze of roads. "This is the tunnel system." He tapped the console and purple lit an area to the far side. "That's where the prison was."

"You keep referring to it as if it doesn't exist anymore," she noted.

"They closed it down years ago because it cost too much to maintain and they weren't receiving monetary help from other planets whose criminals they held."

"Seems fair to me," she replied. "What's the plan?"

He stood her up, turned her around, and straddled her over his lap to relish the heat of her pussy over his hardening dick. She pushed down and wiggled, drawing a moan from him. He wanted to drop her onto her back on the console and pound into her until his name screamed from her throat. A shiver went through him.

"Maybe we have time for a quick one," he said.

Her hands slid down to his waistband when a voice came over the speakers. "HMS Righter, do you request clearance to enter

Clovestea air space?"

Tular fumbled with switches. "Sorry, Clovestea, requesting clearance." Rani giggled and wiggled on his lap again. "It'll have to wait, you little temptress."

Through the speakers came "What was that, HMS Righter?"

He felt his face heat. "Nothing. HMS Righter out." He tapped on the disconnect icon several times, then swatted her ass. "Go put something on that before I tap it again," he said, rubbing her plump globe. "Something shabby, we're laborers looking for work in the yards."

"Oh," she said, "bring extra credits. We may need them."

Twenty minutes later, he and Rani stood in front of the intake desk in the planet tunnels. "Reason for arriving," she said.

"Looking for work. Both male and female types."

The woman stared at Rani, then wrote notes on her clipboard. "We'll place you in the forest and her on the retail side." He nodded an approval. "There are two rooms remaining for the night, choose one. We'll ship you out in the morning."

"Yes, ma'am. Thank you—"

"Next!"

Tular took Rani's hand and headed in the direction the lady indicated.

Rani smiled. "I love how you negotiated separate rooms for us," she said. His hand tightened around her.

"Sorry, babe. You're stuck with me for a long time," he whispered back. If he had his way, it would be forever.

A cart loaded with cleaning supplies, towels, and toilet paper sat in the hallway. The open door next to it was to a vacant room, but the bed sheets needed changing and the bathroom probably needed cleaning.

"You want to wait for the other room or go on in here?"

"Let's go on in," she answered. "I want to talk to the cleaning lady when she comes in."

He stepped inside. "What about?"

She smiled at him. "Watch and listen how it's done, bounty boy." He didn't even want to ask what she was talking about. He trusted she knew what she was doing. Stripping the bed, Rani separated the blankets from the sheets and released the pillows from their covers. He wished there was more time, the bed could be put to better use.

"You know," he said, "there's a woman who will be here any minute to do that."

"I know," she replied, "this is part of the plan."

He let her go about her business. He needed to plot out their next steps. He knew the prison was at the far end of the tunnel system and would take a long time to get to on foot. He also knew Shadowsoul's men would be on guard even if they thought they were safe from detection.

First off, he needed to verify the men were really in the prison. He'd be pissed if it was a trap. Second, they'd need a way to get close to the tunnel guard without getting shot. Then a ton of other logistics. All this could take days.

A knock came from the door. "House cleaning," called a female. Rani jumped off the bed and opened the door while he remained at the small table in the corner.

Rani welcomed the woman inside.

"Thank you so much for taking care of our room."

The lady stared at her. "It's my job." She sounded none too happy to be there.

Rani took the sheets from her hands. "I'm aware of that, but it doesn't mean I'm not appreciative." She set the sheets on the bedside table and picked up the sheet with the stretchy corners. He noted how neatly the sheet was folded. He could never in his entire bachelorhood fold that damn sheet to get it to look nice. He always ended up simply wadding it into a mess.

Rani shook the material free of itself and whipped it across the bed to settle mostly over the mattress. The cleaning lady hadn't moved from her spot. Rani glanced at her. "Would you like to help me?"

The woman snapped out of her daze and shimmied along the side of the bed. "Sorry," the maid said. "I just haven't had anyone volunteer to help."

"It's fine," Rani replied, "I bet you'd rather be home. It's getting late here."

The lady snorted. "Isn't that the truth."

"You have any children?" his new girlfriend asked. He wondered if Rani was this chatty with everyone. What was this "plan" she mentioned? He hoped they hurried. He and Rani would need to sneak out and look for answers before it got much later. They had only a couple hours before the sun went down. There was so much they needed to pull this off.

He glanced at the women and saw Rani hugging a crying cleaning lady. What the hell happened?

"I know," Rani said. "I'd like to help you more." She stretched her hand back to him and gave him grabby fingers. He had no idea what she was doing. She looked over her shoulder at him and mouthed "credits." Oh, she wanted paper credits. He unzipped the hidden pocket in his boot and pulled out a decent amount. What was she going to do with it?

"Here," she said to the woman, "take this." Rani put the credits into the woman's shaking hands.

The maid shoved them back and sniffled. "I can't take your credits. If you're here, you're just like me, scrounging where we can."

Rani refused. "We are fine. Your little girl needs that medical care more than we need this." The woman wiped her nose on her apron and hugged Rani again. "Now that that's settled, let's finish the bed then start the bathroom." The woman nodded and returned to her side of the bed.

Rani picked up the other sheet and tossed it into the air to unfold. She said, "I bet you overhear a lot of things in this job."

"Ha," the lady said, "you have no idea how others go on like I'm not even there. Just an hour ago, I was mopping the aisle outside the bay, and a bunghole jacker told me to stop until after he passed. Then he continued talking to the bay coordinator about the prison and the supplies that needed to be delivered by tomorrow morning."

Rani asked, "This bunghole, was he growling and angry looking?"

"He was."

Rani glanced at him. The lady confirmed that Murrow Zul and the prisoners were there. That was easy enough. But they still had other things to find out.

"I thought the prison was closed down," Rani said.

"It has been for a long time. Only the administration section and a few cells have been reactivated. That's what I heard, anyway."

Well, he thought, that was nice to know. The ladies disappeared into the bathroom. A few minutes later, they came out giggling.

"I'll be right back," the cleaning lady whispered with a sneaky smile and excited eyes. Rani closed the door and plopped back on the bed.

"What was that all about?" he asked.

"Nothing much, she's just getting us tunnel inspector uniforms and a transport to drive to the prison."

His jaw dropped. "How—what—" On second thought. . . "I don't want to know." She laughed and hopped onto his lap and kissed him. Now this, he could get into. He scooted her closer to feel her pressed against his dick. Just when it was getting good, another knock sounded. Rani jumped up and hurried across the room to open the door.

The same female who cleaned their room handed his girl clothes, hats, clipboards and other stuff.

"Thank you so much, Daniyela," Rani whispered.

The maid hugged Rani then held her at arm's length. "I thank you for my daughter's health. Now, go rescue your men and kick that bunghole jacker's ass for me."

"You got it," Rani said. Daniyela closed the door and Rani turned to him, all smiles. "You just have to know the trick," she said to his astounded expression.

Now all he had to do was keep her safe for the next two hours. He wondered if any rope for strapping a woman to a bed was included with all she had.

SIXTEEN

"Ugh! This waiting is killing me." Rani sat on the couch with an exhale. "And your constant calm is annoying as hell."

Tular smirked. "Not the patient kind, are you?"

"You just figure that out, alien boy?" A smirk played on her lips as well.

"You know, there are ways to pass the time, Rani. Stress relievers. Guaranteed." He put the walkie-talkie in his hand on the table and then muted the laptop, his eyes on her the whole time.

"You don't say?" she replied, licking her lips as he walked toward her. The man may have been an alien race, but right now he was molten hotness and as hard and human as any seasoned warrior she'd met, only better.

Tular slid onto the couch beside her, letting his hand skim her thigh. "Yup, definitely guaranteed."

Rani swallowed at the feel of his hand on her thigh. "You've tried this stress reliever before?"

He nodded leaning in to brush his lips against hers. "Practiced and perfected."

"You don't say."

His lips curved above hers. "You said that already."

"So I did. How about you show me?" She slid her hand behind his head and urged his mouth to hers.

He kissed her softly at first, letting his tongue fan the seam of her lips before demanding more. She moaned, opening for the onslaught.

Tular dug his hand into her hair, letting the other rest at her waist as he plundered her mouth. His lips feathered over Rani's chin and across her jaw to the tender skin beneath and she gasped as he pulled her against him.

His body was a hard muscled line and she shivered, feeling dampness spread in her crotch. How they got to this point still stunned her. Tular was a colleague. An ally. And this definitely fell under the banner of fraternization.

"Mmmm…I could taste you all night," he murmured against her lips again, the flicker from the muted laptop sending small shadows against the darkened walls.

His words, almost as much as the feel of his tongue, sent her lower body jerking just thinking of his body and the thrill it promised. Her legs felt liquid at the thought of him plundering her pussy with his hand and his mouth and she was immediately grateful she was sitting.

The feeling of anticipation was enough to make her moan. This time she knew the apex would match the buildup. Sex was usually a disappointment once the act was said and done, leaving her wondering why the hard sell. A means to an end. All deposit. No dividend. In this case, she knew the man knew how to deliver.

Tular's lips continued kissing the concave of her throat, his hand skimming over her breasts from her waist. He squeezed her nipple through her shirt and she gasped at the rough feel even as the soft bud hardened beneath the fabric.

"I want to taste all of you, Rani. Every inch of your silky skin." Without hesitation, he unbuttoned her shirt, trailing his fingers over the swell of her breasts.

He unclipped the front of her bra, freeing her tits. Cupping their weight, he dipped his head to her bare nipples, sucking them between his lips. Rani arched, and he drew the stiffening nubs deeper, one at a time.

"Delicious. You taste as good as you smell, girl. Does your pussy taste as sweet?"

Rani's head spun, and she could barely nod. "Only one way to find out," she croaked.

Skating his hand over her hip, he unbuttoned her pants, helping her shimmy them to the floor. One by one, he removed her boots, slipping her pants from her ankles with a single pull.

He cupped her pussy through her panties, stroking her slit. "You're so wet, baby. Your lace is soaked." His tongue played along her breast as he slid her panties from her as well.

"Spread yourself for me." He slid one knee between hers and climbed between her legs.

Cracking a smile, she pushed at his sculpted chest, stopping him. "It's been a really long time since I've found myself in a situation like this, and with the coming conflict, who knows if I'll ever have the chance again. I want the full treatment. Every delicious, tantalizing visual. So strip."

He got to his feet and kicked off his boots. Reaching for his shirt, he pulled it over his head and dropped it to the floor. His eyes never left hers as he slowly unbuckled his pants, pushing them from his hips to his thighs.

The man's long corded cock sprang free, and Rani licked her lips watching the large member as he pushed his pants the rest of the way to the ground. In seconds, he knelt between her thighs again.

She moaned as his hard head brushed against her soft folds, and she braced for his utter size. He took her mouth instead. He teased her lips and tongue, tempting her throbbing clit with the tip of his cock. "What do you want, Rani? My cock or my mouth?"

Sinking her hands into his hair, she concentrated on his lips and tongue. "Kiss me deep, Tular. Like you've never wanted anyone more. Then fuck me like you own me."

He devoured her lips and she tightened her grip on his hair. His cock jerked as she strained for contact.

He bit her lip, grazing the soft flesh with his teeth. Dropping his hand to her bare breast, he pinched her nipple hard. She sucked in a hiss at the playful pain. "You like it a little rough, Rani? If I fuck you like I own you, you'd better."

"Fuck me, Tular."

Tular shook his head. "I'm not done with you yet."

With a low rumble he broke their kiss. A grin tugged at his lips as he knelt up, pressing the satin of his swollen head to her lips. "I want your mouth wrapped around my dick. Take me deep."

Her lips parted and she inhaled, slipping his engorged head over her tongue. Tular pushed his member to the back of her throat. "Work my shaft, baby. Circle your palm over my head, slick and wet."

Rani took his full length, and a moan left Tular's throat, raw and full of need. "Faster baby. Tongue my balls and work my length."

She ran the flat of her tongue over the corded base of his cock and then sucked his head between her lips again, her teeth grazing his sensitive flesh.

"Oh babe, you're gonna make me blow," he groaned as she released him again.

She smirked, giving his head a quick lick, taking the pearl of cum from the top. "I thought that was the plan of attack."

Tular's entire body went rigid and his cock flexed hard and unyielding in her hand. "You're so damn sexy right now I could cum all over your tongue."

She took his cock deep once more, but then pulled back when he tried to buck his hips, letting him go with a pop. With a frustrated grunt, he pushed her back against the couch. "Two can play at that game."

Pulling her legs up, her ass slid down. He pushed her knees wide, positioning her wet pussy prone and buried his face in her. He licked and sucked, drawing her clit between his teeth.

Rani arched as he slipped two fingers through her slick cleft. Curling his hand, he worked her spot while his thumb circled her hard nub, rubbing and teasing.

"Tular!" She lifted her hips, pushing her pussy farther into his hand.

"It's either fuck me or suck me, Rani. Where do you want my load? In your mouth or in your pussy?"

"Fuck!" With a ragged breath, she fisted his hair as spasms took her lower body. Her walls clenched his hand as she climaxed. Aftershocks sent gooseflesh across her wet thighs. She held herself, muscles tight as Tular continued his slow burn, letting the tension build again.

She sucked in a breath, her head dropping back as another climax crested. Tular pulled his hand back and she grabbed his wrist, but he gripped her thick thighs instead and drove his cock deep. Rani lifted her ass, taking his thick length. She rolled her hips, keeping the frantic grind.

His thick girth filled her past the point of pleasure and pain. Her thighs gripped his hips, her body rigid as her orgasm crashed. She cried out as her walls squeezed his cock tightly inside. Waves took her, her body spasming until her legs went weak even with his dick still rock-hard within.

Tular's ass coiled hard as he pounded her pussy. His gaze was dark and full of need and he held himself taut and unmoving inside her. Her eyes met his as he pulled back one last time, driving his cock fast and deep. Teeth gritted, he let go as hot spurts filled her core.

SEVENTEEN

Dressed in official government uniforms with clipboards holding tunnel inspection forms, Rani and her man walked out a side door to the port to get a large passenger transport with the pass card Daniyela provided. Without a word from anyone, they drove off.

Rani's heart broke for the woman's situation. Dani worked two jobs to feed her daughter and buy desperately needed medicine for her weak lungs. The child was born prematurely, and the father had abandoned Dani when she told him she was pregnant. The little bit of credits Rani gave her allowed Dani to pay the rent she would be short because of taking off days for her daughter's medical appointments. It was the least Rani could do.

But maybe there was more. In the past two days, she'd met three woman who were in unique positions that made getting information easy and effective. And that was without them even trying. With some training and monetary motivation, perhaps these women would like to belong to a group who gathered intel and acted on it to help others.

Rani could start her own galactic investigation agency to bring the bad guys to justice and prevent things like the prince's abduction. Even Tular could be a part. With his bounty hunting experience, he'd be a perfect fit to not only capture dungholes, but train the women.

These ideas made her super excited. A new beginning that let her keep doing the things she loved and helped out other women with extra credits and a sense of purpose. She wanted to share her ideas with Tular, but someone stood in the middle of the tunnel ahead of them. Time to use her sucky acting skills again. Maybe she'd stay in the cart.

Tular stopped the transport when the man standing in the tunnel pulled his gun out. Clipboard in hand, he got out and walked up to the guard. She followed behind. The men's voices were low at first, then Tular sighed loudly.

"Look, sir, if this can't be started tonight, I'll have to call the main station and get everyone up in arms and then the delegates and all their servants will come out here—"

As Tular continued his dramatic monologue, Rani pulled the butterfly clip from her pocket and pulled off the cap. With a quick stab to the arm, the sharp needle penetrated the guard's shirt, knocking him out in seconds.

They dragged him around a corner and bound his hands and feet with cords in the transport.

Now to find her men.

Inside, the air was musty from being closed up so long. Everything seemed to be made of metal like the inside of a battlecruiser. Fire wasn't a worry for this place. When Tular caught up, he took her hand and gave her a silent scold. She raised a brow at him. If that look was because she went in first, then they would have a serious talk after this. She was not waiting for anyone to babysit her.

A quite unexpected and delicious smell reached them. Tular and she followed the aroma to the kitchens. They stepped inside and a voice rang out. "It's about time!"

Rani jumped in a half circle to face a woman in a white chef's coat glaring at them. The woman went on with her yelling. "Aprons are in the closet. We need three boxes of anbraug from the delivery room. Get those first."

Rani and Tular glanced at each other. She understood the question on his face—do you want to play along? Being the kitchen help made more sense than tunnel inspectors at this point. She gave a small nod.

"Go, go!" the chef hollered. "What are you waiting for?"

They hurried toward the closet, grabbed two white smocks and hair coverings then hurried out the door. "Which way is the delivery dock, do you think?" she asked Tular.

"My guess would be close to where we came in. They'd have to bring in supplies through the tunnels, not above ground." They ran along the narrow aisle back the way they came and quickly came upon a busy bay-like area. Transports were backed in and being unloaded. Food for a full army of men were spread on pallets and set against walls. She saw a picture of the root plant they were looking for and pointed.

"There. Take two and I'll get one," she said. They snatched up boxes, and a familiar gruff growling sound stopped them in their steps. Murrow Zul was in the bay and had seen them.

"Halt," Murrow ordered, but they had already stopped. "Bring the woman to me." Her eyes told Tular to chill out. She had this under control. A guard yanked her toward Murrow. She held onto her box of plants, crossed her eyes, and snarled a lip for good effect.

Murrow stared her up and down. "Do I know you?" he asked.

"No," Rani said in a high voice. He stared at her longer. Sweat broke on her forehead, her knees were starting to buckle. "We're here to help in the kitchens. If we don't get back soon, the chef will be angry and I don't want it at me."

Zul mumbled something under his breath. "Fine," he raised an arm, "go." She and Tular hurried off. That was not fun.

Back in the kitchen, the two assessed the situation as they peeled anbraug. "Got any ideas?" he asked.

"Their first course is soup. I'll drop some sleep agent in each bowl and they'll be out. We'll have the run of the place." They watched as the cook taste-tested the broth and smiled.

"Prepare the bowls!" the woman yelled. Both she and Tular searched for bowls, finally coming upon dust-crusted dishes. After a quick wash down, they doled out equal portions of both liquids, one from a pot, the other from her pin, and Tular loaded the bowls onto a rolling cart. The chef returned with her hair fixed and makeup adjusted. Rani glanced at Tular and he shrugged.

Rani, following the woman, pushed the cart into the dining room. Shadowsoul's men continued talking like the females hadn't appeared. She listened as they talked about the prince and the credits they intended to collect and what they were going to do with it all.

Another guard walked in and took a seat.

"The prince secured?" Murrow asked.

"In the first cell block," the guard said.

Murrow turned to another. "What about the Guardians?"

A slimy piece of gundur shit smiled. "They are being locked in the cage as we speak. Fresh blood spread around the area to call the beasts nearby."

Murrow chuckled. "Stupid dungholes. They should know the inhabitants are loyal to Shadowsoul. They will never betray him."

Soups were served and sipped. The entire time, Rani felt Murrow's eyes on her. Twice, he'd seen her in her makeup, the last brief time was with her real face before Tular showed up. When all the dishes were served, the chef handed Rani the drink container with instructions to refill mugs then left. Starting on the opposite side of the table from Zul, she poured, trying to keep her hands from shaking. That would be a dead giveaway of fear, and fear a lot of times came from worry of being caught.

Eyes started closing, heads bobbing. Rani backed away with a gasp when the guy next to her fell from his chair.

With an animal-like roar, Murrow Zul

sprung from his chair, weapon pointed at her. "I remember you now. How are you. . . you. . ." A bolt shot from his gun, going wide, and he fell to the floor. Tular darted through the entrance, his eyes frantic to find her.

"I'm okay," she hollered. "My guys are in the cage," she said. "Where is that?"

He answered, "It's outside. It's where they put criminals with a death decree. They are eaten by the monster creatures on the planet's surface. There is little hope for them, especially if they spilled blood around the perimeter. The monsters would be only minutes from reaching them. Where is the prince?"

"They said he's in the first cell block," she answered. Tular turned to leave. "Wait," Rani called out. "You're not helping me get my men first. They are going to die. The prince is safe."

Sadness filled his eyes. "I'm sorry, Rani. You don't understand my obligation. Your men may already be dead." He ran from her.

"Oh, I understand your obligation to riches. That's all your kind is loyal to, you piece of worm shit." She picked up Murrow's weapon. "I don't need you. I don't want to ever see your face again."

Rani remembered from the diagram where the tunnel was leading to the surface. It wasn't too far from the administration side of the prison. Instead of being a porthole with metal rungs to climb up, this was a set of stairs to a low-ceiling ramp that exited into the waning hours of light. The entrance was just high enough to drive a transport through.

From the ramp's edge, she saw her men lying on the ground inside a metal cage, the bars bent and broken as if they had been torn apart and put back together. The men were covered in blood and there were puddles of it all over the place. Then she remembered the smell and how it drew the land's toothy natives. The ground vibrated under her feet. The creatures were coming.

EIGHTEEN

On the underground section of the ramp leading out to the wilderness, Rani searched the abandoned work area for keys or something to get her team out of the cage. From a wall panel she forced open, she snatched up what could be a key and ran the distance to the cage.

Sagestar called out, "Rani, how are you here?" He dragged himself with his arms, his legs seemingly injured.

"We need to get everyone out of here and inside," she said. "Deadly animals are coming to eat you."

"What?!" her comrade yelled. He turned. "Sergeant—"

"I heard her, Sagestar," Sid hollered. "Ignore her. Let's get the men inside."

Rani pulled the gate back, and the men stumbled through, helping each other. Ironwin lay in a puddle of blood. She ran in to him.

"What happened?" Rani asked, tears in her eyes for a beloved team member.

"Nothing much, boss lady," Ironwin wheezed. It sounded like his lungs were filled with liquid—probably blood. Rani wrapped his arm over her shoulder and hauled him to his feet. The ground vibrated stronger, causing her steps to become unbalanced.

"Why do you call me that?" she asked Kase.

He chuckled then groaned, almost going to a knee, but she kept him moving. His voice was barely louder than a breath. "You remind me too much of my sister I lost in a raid on our village before we moved to Depleon. To keep from overprotecting you and to remind myself you aren't her, I call you *boss* to keep my grief in check."

At the end of his story, tears poured down her cheeks. Maybe he wasn't as much of a kid as she thought. He was someone trying to find all the joy in life that he could, knowing it could be gone in seconds.

Close to the ramp, one of the other men took Ironwin and she ran back to the cage to help anyone else. Seeing no one, she turned and slammed into Sid's chest. She bounced backward and fell inside the cage. He slammed the door on her and stood outside the wall glaring at her. The vibrations were closer and stronger.

He sneered at her. "Well, little woman, look who's on the inside and who's on the outside."

Rani climbed to her feet. "You know, Sid, you made your own life and that of those around you miserable because you just can't let things go. Do you think that woman beating you for whatever meant it personally? She probably didn't give a rangtoo's ass who you were. She was going to do the best she could, and it happened to be a bit better than you."

Sid slammed his fist into the wall fencing. Rani didn't blink. He stepped back, his face turning redder than her lip-fluffing lipstick. His hands balled into fists as he yelled at the top of his lungs. Spittle flew from his mouth and his rage shook him.

She half-listened as he vented and felt in her pocket for the key. She needed to get away from him before he attracted too much attention.

She knelt and patted dirt on her sleeves to make her shirt lighter and hopefully dull her blood scent. Sid continuing yelling. Her eyes skimmed the area. The ground's shaking had stopped and that worried her. Sid kept up his tirade, now yelling at her for not paying attention to him.

Movement from the side caught her eye. A reptilian head with a huge mouth and lots of teeth rose above the trees on a neck that kept going and going. The head swooped toward her and Sid. She fell to the ground, and Sid turned to see what she was gaping at.

The beast bit down on the top half of Sid's body and tossed him a hundred feet into the air, its neck straightening to catch the sergeant's body in its mouth like tossing a corn kernel into the air and catching it in your mouth. It was suddenly quiet.

The animal sniffed around the area, but there was so much blood everywhere, it must not have smelled her. It head knocked against the cage, the bent bars crashing around her. She sucked in a breath, waiting and praying it would go away. After long, tense moments, it sniffed a final time before stomping away.

Rani cranked the key in the lock and ran for the ramp where her team sat quiet and in shock.

"Is everybody able to move? We have a short distance to the transport. It probably has a med kit." The guys looked bad, clothes torn and dried blood everywhere. "What in the—did they do this to you?" she asked.

Sagestar replied, "Their leader, Murrow Zul, said no one would get in his way for getting revenge for his sister who was killed on Sathides."

She'd heard that planet's name before. "That's where the prince is from."

Her teammate nodded. "That's the whole point. Zul abducted the prince with Shadowsoul's permission and planned to torture him to get vengeance for his sister's death."

"So this has nothing to do with Shadowsoul, himself, huh?" she asked.

"Not really," Sagestar said. Oh well, she

thought. Shadow was a bad guy who needed to die anyway for all the women he'd killed after pampering them. She could only shake her head.

"Let's go, guys," she said, picking up the weapon she'd dropped before running to the cage. "Some of Zul's men are inside, but we have them sedated right now. We'll get you to the tunnel and to a med bay."

Remaining as quiet as possible, Rani led them through the halls until coming around a corner and seeing Tular standing next to the prince, both with hands up and a guard pointing a weapon at them.

Then the truth was finally revealed. He'd lied to her. Flat out, bald-faced lied about everything.

NINETEEN

Tarrek entered the cell area with trepidation flowing through him. He hadn't seen the crown prince of Sathides or the rest of his family in a decade. But he knew he had no choice. When he'd learned of the death of Murrow Zul's sister on his home planet, he hightailed it to Drace's planet to see if any plans had been in the works for retaliation.

Disguised as a dockworker, and then a guard, he worked his way in to get intel, but he seemed always a step behind. And then he met Rani who seemed to get the same information in one afternoon that took him days. He had overheard her and the waitress talking in the restaurant and wanted to know what she did.

Not only did he get to know what she did, but he got to know her and fell hard for someone who was perfect for him, meant for him.

And now he'd lost her because he hadn't gotten around to telling her the truth. Hopefully she'd listen to him when this was all over and would understand why he chose as he did. Not only did his family depend on him, but an entire planet. Plus, there was a bit of a selfish reason for saving his brother.

He grabbed keys in the control room before entering the cell block. His boots echoed in the empty space of the square. He heard shuffling and movement in the confined room he approached. With his next step, he went to his knee as a sharp piece of metal flew out from between the cell bars aimed where his heart would've been had he been standing.

He laughed. "Phrey," he said, "you were always noisy when it came to that move."

The prince gasped, and Tular stepped up to the bars. He looked into the eyes of his only sibling, in many, many years.

He said, "How you've been, Phrey?" His brother stood several paces from the front and didn't move or say anything, surprise evident on his face. He looked a little roughed up, dirty, but not as bad as he had after the night of his turning an adult—the crown prince coming of age. He and his brother partied unlike anything that had occurred on the planet in a century.

When Phrey didn't reply, Tular sighed and realized nothing had changed. The family still rejected him for not wanting to be part of the politics that separated their planet into warring factions. He believed change was needed to adapt with the times. But his father and brother wanted to stick with tradition. Tradition had worked until it didn't.

Instead of betraying himself, Tular left. He couldn't do what he didn't believe in.

He opened the jail's door and walked away. His brother could find his way out, and he needed to find Rani and make things right between them. If her men were still alive, maybe he could help get them out.

Tular felt a hand on his shoulder and turned. Next he knew, his brother delivered an uppercut to his jaw, making Tular step back.

"That is for making Mom cry every night for two weeks," Phrey said, anger in his voice. Tular had no doubts on that. She would've missed him like any mother would. Before he could say anything, his brother wrapped his arms around him. "And this is for never forgetting about family."

Tular hugged his big brother, holding back tears he'd never admit to. He held his tongue, afraid his voice would crack. After a moment, he was able to talk. "Just because I don't believe in tradition doesn't mean I love my family any less."

His brother's eyes turned away. "Would it make you feel any better if I told you, you were right?"

Tular laughed. "I already knew I was." Phrey grunted at him. "It's fine, big brother," Tular said. "You had little say being the next in line. I, on the other hand, had no such weight hanging over me. I saw things you never could. Besides, if I'd grown up as big a sissy as you, who would've rescued you?"

Phrey grunted again. "Remember that when you meet with the council."

"I don't think so," Tular replied. "I don't have a death wish." He gestured for his brother to follow him out. "Besides, back when I promised not to tell Mom about you and Morna Stillwater being caught together, you said you'd always go to council so I wouldn't have to."

"Well, that doesn't work anymore. Guess who I married," Phrey said. Tular laughed and slapped him on the back.

Around a corner in front of them stepped a guard with a weapon pointed. Both royals froze, hands up. The guard snarled at them. "You killed all of them." He lifted his weapon.

"Who?" Tular asked, knowing he'd never killed anyone.

"All the Shadow men," the guard said. Tular stepped in front of his brother and was surprised when his brother fought him to see who took the kill shot. Both cringed when a shot rang out.

Not feeling any pain, Tular patted his hands over his brother who was doing the same to him.

"You two can play handsies later," a female voice said from the aisle behind where the guard stood. A very familiar and loved female voice. Tular saw the dead guard, face down, and Rani with several men farther back in the hall.

"Someone you know?" Phrey asked.

"Maybe. Hopefully," Tular said, wondering if Rani would talk to him. The groups met in the middle and turned down the hall the guard came from.

"Who is the dead guy?" she asked.

"Never saw him with the others," Tular said. "He must've been on duty when the rest were eating." Quick introductions were made, and the new group made their way to the transport outside the prison entrance.

Rani led them out and found the med kit.

Phrey leaned into Tular. "You picked a good one, brother. I believe she could hold her own even with Father."

Tular smiled. "I'd be more worried about Mother."

Rani suddenly stood and looked toward the entrance. She passed her patient to one of the guys and headed for the prison doors.

"Rani," Tular called out, running up to her. "Where are you going?"

"I'm getting the chef. We can't leave her. When Zul wakens, he'll kill her if she's still there. He probably thinks she's with us."

"Then I'm coming with you," he said. He expected her to argue because she was angry with him for lying to her.

She poked him in the chest. "Yes, I'm angry at you, but I understand why you did what you did. And if you lie to me again, I will so kick your ass."

He kissed her long and hard. Damn, he loved this woman. "I swear never to lie to you again." She was sexy as hell when she was bossy.

"Good, let's go." She led him into the kitchen and found it empty. Stepping back into the hall, they heard noise coming from one of the rooms. They hurried to the door and found the cook trying to work dusty electronics resembling communication devices of old.

"Chef," he said, "come out with us. We'll take you back to town."

The woman picked up a pan and spun around. "Who are you?" she asked.

"I'm Prince Tular Leighton from the planet Sathides, here to rescue my brother who these men abducted."

"And I'm Rani Kerf, Guardian from

Depleon, here to rescue my team and the prince."

The chef's brows raised at Rani. "You? A Guardian?" His woman rolled her eyes. He laughed and headed toward the door. Stepping out, a searing pain hit him in the stomach. He glanced up to see Murrow leaning against a wall, then he was jerked sideways and the door slammed shut.

Rani was over him as he lay on the floor. "Tular, you've been shot. Don't move."

TWENTY

Rani froze at the sound of a laser blast and stopped breathing when she saw Tular double over. She dragged him inside and slammed the door closed. As any good prison design, the walls were strong enough to keep out normal weapon fire, so she locked the door and attended to Tular.

The chef pulled off her coat and they folded it to press against the open wound in his torso. "Tular, you've been shot. Don't move." She looked at the equipment. "Chef, was anything working?"

"No, not a sound."

"Okay." Rani took a deep breath. She had to find a way to get them out of this room with a madman holding a gun outside the door.

"Come out, Leighton," Murrow said from a distance. "And I'll let you live."

Rani took the only choice she had. Opening the door a bit, she yelled out, "He's dead. You shot him."

He chuckled. "Come on out then, female."

"Why?!" she hollered. "You'll just shoot me too!"

"You can bet your sweet ass I will if I have to come in there and get you."

She closed the door, knowing he meant what he said. The only hope they had was for her to distract Murrow while the chef got Tular to the men out the doors.

"Here's the plan, chef." Rani explained her impromptu idea. Everything was ready when Tular grabbed her arm.

"No, you can't go out there," he whispered.

"He's not going to hurt me. He has no reason," Rani replied.

"He does," Tular breathed. "He's the one who kills Shadowsoul's women when Drace tells him to take them back to the port."

That got her attention. "Why?" she asked.

The chef answered for him. "Why does any piece of shit need a reason to do what they do?"

True, but Rani had no choice. She leaned down and kissed him, knowing this might be the last time she ever saw him. "I love you," she said. "I know it hasn't been long enough, but you know when it's right, and you're right for me. That is why I'm doing this."

She got to her feet and put a hand on the door. "Remember," Rani said to the chef, "he doesn't know you are in here. Wait till I get him far enough away." With that, she opened the door and slowly stepped out.

Murrow leaned against the wall, barely able to keep his eyes open. Each moment she delayed, the more awake he'd become. With her hands up, she slowly moved toward him. He looked her up and down and smiled. Revulsion rolled through her. She tried to hide it, but his grimace said she didn't do well.

When she was close, he reached out to grab her hand. In a move similar to what she practiced with Ironwin in the gym not two days ago, she swept Murrow's arm to the side and delivered a kick to his balls.

He fell to his knees but held fast to his gun. There was no place she could run where the laser bolt wouldn't find her. He raised the gun, then a beam of light sizzled into the side of his head, knocking him onto his back. Rani glanced in the direction the shot came from, seeing one of Sid's guys with a weapon. Her stomach churned.

This was the perfect opportunity for the men on the team who disapproved of her to get rid of her for good. She wondered if gender equality would ever be accepted universally. Everyone had strengths and weaknesses and contributed in their own way. Apparently, Sid's guys never saw that. Unbelieving, she watched as a smile spread across his face.

"Come on, Kerf," he said, "Sagestar said to gather the whole team. You've more than earned a spot with us. We'd be dead if not for you. You're getting a medal for this. The first for a trainee ever."

She spun on her heel. "Thanks, but we have a medical emergency. Get the guys ready to go."

An hour later, Humphrey had Tular in the best medical care the planet had. They would have him patched up and as good as new.

In the meantime, Rani's crew went through triage and headed back to the ship. Each male who sneered at her earlier shook her hand, apologizing for their treatment. They agreed to not underestimate women again. Muscle didn't solve everything.

TWENTY-ONE

Rani and her team stood on the steps in front of the Royal Houses on the planet Sathides. Each of them wore a medal of honor around their neck for exceptional bravery in rescuing the crown prince.

Tular's father, who she met briefly, was at the podium praising the Guardians for a job well done and making them the official protectors of Sathides, which didn't mean much to her. She had her own ideas of where she was headed next and it wasn't with the Guardians.

She had plans for her own agency with women, and men, to gather intel and use it to help others in trouble. Another option was to help the Guardians expand. She hadn't decided which way to go yet. She already had three women who wanted to sign on. Jordyna, Arbelle, and Daniyela would make great initial teammates.

When the king and prince were finished with their speeches, Tular stepped up to the podium, dressed in royal attire. She had to admit she liked him better in his other clothes. The royal garb did nothing to show off his arms, abs, or ass.

She noticed him glancing at her when her eyes were on his ass. Oops. His face blushed a bit, but it was warm out so no one would guess why.

"I'd also like to say a few words before you go." Someone in the massive crowd yelled out that it was nice to have him home. He chuckled. "It's nice to be home." He glanced at his family lined up beside him. Rani's heart melted, knowing how they were once again a family, willing to put aside differences to work together for the good of their planet.

Tular continued. "As you all know, the Guardians were instrumental in bringing my brother home safely. I can't thank them enough. But there is one in particular I'd like to mention."

Rani's face paled. He never said anything about telling everyone what really happened. It was decided that the Guardians, with assistance from Tular, had rescued the prince and killed a few in the process—and lost one of their own, Sgt. Sid Booth, whose body was never found.

"This person stepped up when duty called and went beyond what any one person could ever be asked to do. Their life was on the line, time and time again. And she helped me to see that sometimes things worked out for a reason and when they didn't, you had to make them work.

"She is the bravest being I've ever met, and she voluntarily laid her life down for mine. But fortunately, it didn't come to that. So that is why. . ." he pulled something small from his royal robe pocket. Rani couldn't see what it was since she was at the end of the line.

He restarted. "That is why I'm asking her to marry me."

Rani gasped along with the crowd. He smiled as he came toward her, small container in his hand. He knelt in front of her before all his planet and asked her to be with him forever.

* * *

"Are you okay?" Tular asked, watching Rani as she took in the polished chrome and silk of the royal chamber.

She nodded, but clearly wasn't paying much attention. "Yeah," she replied absently. "This place is off the hook. It's a cross between Star Trek and a medieval castle!"

"It's a blend, I guess. Old and new with a touch of technology." He came up behind her and slipped his hands onto her shoulders. "Either way, you improve it." Tular moved her hair to one side and kissed her neck. "It's home...for now."

Rani turned in his arms. "For now, huh. Does that mean we get our own castle of chrome and stone, or do you plan on whisking me away to some far-off place just to get me alone?"

"We are alone, silly." He kissed her before giving her nose a quick peck.

"I don't know about that. This place is so sci-fi on steroids you could have bots melded into the walls or furniture that track your every whim…your every need."

He laughed, walking her backward toward the round, silk covered bed. "My every need, huh." The back of her knees hit the edge of the mattress and Tular skimmed his hand to hers, moving it to his crotch. "The only need I have now is to bury my cock so deep inside you, you scream for release."

"Really." She molded her hand around the hard bar of his cock.

He took her mouth and kissed her, hungry and greedy. "All I've done since you agreed to be my wife is imagine your sweet ass and how many ways I can tap it."

"And how many is that?" she asked, giving his hard length a squeeze.

In one move he grabbed her waist and tossed her over his shoulder, not bothering with an answer. He turned toward what looked like a solid chrome wall, only to have the center part exposing a sumptuous bathroom. He walked through the door, letting her slide down his muscled chest.

"I thought a hot shower would help us both relax, considering," he said, his voice low and as intense as the look in his eyes.

"Another relaxation strategy?" She giggled, but her breath still caught at the thought of his cock and how it filled her to the point of pleasure insanity.

"When it comes to your body, I will never be that relaxed." He pressed a series of button on the wall beside the dual vanities and hot spray poured from the showerhead in the sunken bath. "Ladies first."

Rani licked her lips and took a step back, peeling her clothes off in a sexy strip tease. She dropped each item in a trail, her hips moving in a sensual sway. He shrugged out of his shirt and dropped it to the floor before pushing his pants to the tile.

She stepped into the spray and continued her seduction, letting one hand linger on her breast while the other dipped low over her mound.

"Oh, baby. You are so fucking hot." Stepping out of the circle of clothes, he wrapped his hand around his thick cock.

She stood naked and waiting as Tular swept her into the spray, letting its warmth soak them both. Spinning her around, his hands were on her shoulders again, only this time he pushed her to her knees. He pressed his cock to her lips and fisted her hair. "All of me, baby. Like your favorite lollipop."

With a soft gasp, she sucked him deep. Working his hard length, she ran her palm over his shaft to his head, letting her tongue curl under its ridged edge. Tular tightened his grip on her hair, pushing his dick deeper, and then with a yank he pulled free of her mouth and pulled her to standing.

"Is your pussy as soaked as the rest of you?" he asked, cupping her chin. He leaned in to bite her bottom lip, pulling the tender flesh between his teeth. "Kneel, love. I want you on all fours."

Rani stepped back, putting her hands on her hips. Her breasts ached and her slit was slick with need. "Is that the way you speak to your future royal wife?"

He grinned, pulling her to the wet tile along with him. He slid his hands into her wet hair and took her mouth, hungry again. "It is when I want to fuck her so hard, she comes like a fireball. It is when I want to spread her wide and fuck her luscious royal ass."

Tular's raw words made her gasp and

her clit ache. Her pussy dripped with need, mixing with the shower water trickling between her thighs. She bit his bottom lip, the way he did hers. "Well, since you put it that way." She turned, moving to her hands and knees.

Tular reached between her legs and palmed her slick juice. His thumb circled her clit as her fingers covered his, guiding them into her wet slit.

"So fucking wet. So fucking hot."

She glanced over her shoulder. "Taste me, Tular. I'm drenched for you and only you."

Gripping her hips, he pushed her knees wide and spread her cheeks, dragging his tongue from her pussy to her ass. His fingers plunged into her tight, slick slit while his thumb ringed her tight hole.

She gasped as the pad of his thumb worked her in time with his fingers. She ground her hips back for more, but he pulled his hand away and with a fierce yank, drove his cock into her pussy fast and hard.

He pulled back again, his fingers gripping her flesh as slammed his thick length, balls deep again.

Rani hissed, throwing her head back, her wet hair cascading down her back. "Ahhh! Fuck me, Tular! Harder! I want to feel your balls slap my ass!"

An orgasm ripped through her making his full body throb with need. He reached for her hair and dug his fingers through the wet tangles. Riding her hard, his teeth clenched as she matched each thrust. Her body quaked again, her walls squeezing his thick shaft.

"Come for me, Tular! Fill me."

He snarled. "Oh, I will. I'll stretch you boneless!"

With a grunt, he pulled his cock from her wet cleft and spread her cheeks. With one hand, he spread her slippery juice toward her tight ring. "I told you I want every inch of you, love. Your mouth, your pussy and now your ass. You're wet enough. You're slick enough, and you're ready to burst. One push, baby. That's all it takes. Do you trust me?"

Rani raised her ass high and glanced over her shoulder. "Do it! Hard! Now!"

Pressing his swollen head to her tight hole, he drove his cock deep with one violent thrust. She cried out, as his hand cupped her pussy working her to another climax. Her body sucked his cock in a vise grip. "Tight. So fucking tight."

He pulled back again, driving deep into the snug channel once more. With a low groan, he held still, gripping her hips. "I can't hold much longer, Rani. I'm going to cum, hard. Where do you want it?"

"In my ass! Now!"

Her body clenched and she cried out again. With a rough gulp, his cock pulsed, emptying deep in her tight passage. He held her close, one arm around her waist and the other still cupping her pussy.

"You okay?" he asked.

She shivered. "Me? I'm fine. Just don't ask me to sit anytime soon."

He grinned against her warm, wet skin. "I'll make sure to have a soft cushion handy for your throne, Your Majesty."

EPILOGUE

Rani loved the purple-orange skies of Azaran. Being on her honeymoon on one of the most beautiful planets she'd ever heard of was a dream. She lifted her face to the twin suns and grinned. Her heart was full and soon, things would be a lot more hectic for her and Tular.

"You look beautiful soaking in the sun, love."

She glanced at her new husband and licked her lips. God. This man could do something like make her knees weak with his presence alone. How was that possible? It didn't matter. Because loving him didn't make her weak; it gave her strength.

He'd said he'd support her in whatever

she wanted to do and help her make her way up the ranks, but now that she saw what life was like when finding the person meant to share it with you, she didn't doubt she could achieve anything.

"Thank you."

He pulled her into his arms and kissed her temple. She loved how big and strong he was and how perfect she fit in his arms.

"What for?" he asked.

"For believing in me when I doubted myself."

He cupped her jaw and gave her a deep look. "You're strong, Rani. That's a part of who you are. You can do anything. You've already proven it."

She nodded and hugged him back. Now it was time to show her superiors how strong she really was. It would take time, but eventually, she'd get right to the top. Exactly where she always envisioned herself and other females. Leading the way for the Guardians.

And if the guardians weren't ready for her, then she'd just have to go on to show the universe she could create her own agency. She wasn't limited any longer.

Guardians or not, she was going to see more women out there doing what she loved.

"I love you," she whispered.

"My heart is yours, my love. Now and forever."

ABOUT THE AUTHOR

New York Times and USA Today Bestselling Author

Hi! I'm Milly Taiden. I love to write sexy stories featuring fun, sassy heroines with curves and growly alpha males with fur. My books are a great way to satisfy your craving for contemporary or paranormal romance with action, humor, suspense and happily ever afters.

I live in Florida with my hubby, our boys, and our fur children Speedy, Stormy and Teddy. I am seriously addicted to chocolate and cake.

I love to meet new readers, so come sign up for my newsletter and check out my Facebook page. We always have lots of fun stuff going on there.

SIGN UP FOR MILLY TAIDEN'S NEWSLETTER

FOR LATEST NEWS, GIVEAWAYS, EXCERPTS,

AND MORE!

http://eepurl.com/pt9q1

Find out more about Milly Taiden here:

Email: millytaiden@gmail.com

Website: http://www.millytaiden.com

Facebook:
http://www.facebook.com/millytaidenpage

Twitter: https://www.twitter.com/millytaiden

If you liked this story, you might also enjoy the following by Milly Taiden:

Sassy Mates / Sassy Ever After Series

Scent of a Mate *Book One*

A Mate's Bite *Book Two*

Unexpectedly Mated *Book Three*

A Sassy Wedding *Short 3.7*

The Mate Challenge *Book Four*

Sassy in Diapers *Short 4.3*

Fighting for Her Mate *Book Five*

A Fang in the Sass *Book 6*

Also, check out the **Sassy Ever After World on Amazon at** mtworldspress.com

A.L.F.A Series

Elemental Mating *Book One*

Mating Needs *Book Two*

Dangerous Mating *Book Three*

Fearless Mating *Book Four*

Savage Shifters

Savage Bite *Book One*

Savage Kiss *Book Two*

Savage Hunger *Book Three*

Savage Wedding *Book Four*

Drachen Mates

Bound in Flames *Book One*

Bound in Darkness *Book Two*

Bound in Eternity *Book Three*

Bound in Ashes *Book Four*

Federal Paranormal Unit

Wolf Protector *Federal Paranormal Unit Book One*

Dangerous Protector *Federal Paranormal Unit Book Two*

Unwanted Protector *Federal Paranormal Unit Book Three*

Paranormal Dating Agency

Twice the Growl *Book One*

Geek Bearing Gifts *Book Two*

The Purrfect Match *Book Three*

Curves 'Em Right *Book Four*

Tall, Dark and Panther *Book Five*

The Alion King *Book Six*

There's Snow Escape *Book Seven*

Scaling Her Dragon *Book Eight*

In the Roar *Book Nine*

Scrooge Me Hard *Short One*

Bearfoot and Pregnant *Book Ten*

All Kitten Aside *Book Eleven*

Oh My Roared *Book Twelve*

Piece of Tail *Book Thirteen*

Kiss My Asteroid *Book Fourteen*

Scrooge Me Again *Short Two*

Born with a Silver Moon *Book Fifteen*

Sun in the Oven *Book Sixteen*

Between Ice and Frost *Book Seventeen*

Book Eighteen (Coming Soon)

Also, check out the **Paranormal Dating Agency World on Amazon or at** <u>mtworldspress.com</u>

Raging Falls

Miss Taken *Book One*

Miss Matched *Book Two*

Miss Behaved *Book Three*

Miss Behaved *Book Three*

Miss Mated *Book Four*

Miss Conceived *Book Five (Coming Soon)*

FUR-ocious Lust - Bears

Fur-Bidden *Book One*

Fur-Gotten *Book Two*

Fur-Given Book *Three*

FUR-ocious Lust - Tigers

Stripe-Tease *Book Four*

Stripe-Search *Book Five*

Stripe-Club *Book Six*

Night and Day Ink

Bitten by Night *Book One*

Seduced by Days *Book Two*

Mated by Night *Book Three*

Taken by Night *Book Four*

Dragon Baby *Book Five*

Shifters Undercover

Bearly in Control *Book One*

Fur Fox's Sake *Book Two*

Black Meadow Pack

Sharp Change *Black Meadows Pack Book One*

Caged Heat *Black Meadows Pack Book Two*

Other Works

Wolf Fever

Fate's Wish

Wynter's Captive

Sinfully Naughty Vol. 1

Don't Drink and Hex

Hex Gone Wild

Hex and Kisses

Alpha Owned

Match Made in Hell

Alpha Geek

HOWLS Romances

The Wolf's Royal Baby

The Wolf's Bandit

Goldie and the Bears

Her Fairytale Wolf *Co-Written*

The Wolf's Dream Mate *Co-Written*

Her Winter Wolves *Co-Written*

Contemporary Works

Lucky Chase

Their Second Chance

Club Duo Boxed Set

A Hero's Pride

A Hero Scarred

A Hero for Sale

Wounded Soldiers Set

If you enjoyed the book, please consider leaving a review, even if it's only a line or two; it would make all the difference and would

9 781792 074936